THE COWBOY

A GOODWATER RANCH ROMANCE

AMANDA LEWIS

For my parents,

who seldom watch anything

besides the Western channel

Therefore I say unto you, what things so ever ye desire, when ye pray, believe that ye receive *them*, and ye shall have *them*.

Mark 11:24

At the dawn of the pioneering era, Jedediah Goodwater and his wife Mary packed up and headed West, with nothing to their names but hopes, dreams, and a few cans of beans.

When they got to Louisiana, their bodies parched, their spirits downtrodden, and Mary sick with dysentery, an angel appeared to Jedediah and advised him to leave the beaten trail and head South.

Jedediah didn't know if this was a mirage, or the voice of God himself, but he figured he shouldn't anger anything that was more powerful than him. So, he steered his horse to the left, and down south they headed.

Just a day's ride later, Jedediah started noticing a change in the scenery. No longer were they traveling through a barren wasteland. Lush trees and mountains were coming up all around them. Indeed, a miraculous, undiscovered oasis was what Jedediah and his wife had stumbled upon.

As he pulled the reigns, the weary couple carefully peered over the cliff. Sure enough, what lay before them were the rivers of the Mississippi, Tennessee, and Colorado, all convening to form a waterfall that would make Niagara cry in shame.

Beside themselves with equal parts thirst, exhaustion, and excitement, the couple stumbled down a path in the jagged landscape and dived, from a safe distance, into the pool of *water below them. Savagely, they lapped up the waters, Mary's ailments immediately cured and Jedediah replenished with hydration and a newfound thirst for life.*

They made their homestead right then and there, at the base of those falls, and called it "Goodwater Ranch," because they had, in fact, found some good water.

Soon, word spread like wildfire about Goodwater Ranch, and more and more people migrated. The name stuck, and pretty soon folks were referring to the whole town as Goodwater Ranch.

Nowadays, the original Goodwater Ranch home is the headquarters for the historical society. And the town itself, Goodwater Ranch, Texas, is a very popular attraction, whether it be with the locals who live there all year round, the ailing who come from all over to taste the healing good water, or the tourists who come to see the movie sets and music videos which feature the Goodwater Falls as a backdrop.

No matter where you're from, or what you've been through, everybody finds a home in Goodwater Ranch.

Prologue

He sat on the flat rock overlooking the landscape, extending his hat upwards. The thunder roared overhead, and the gentle *plop, plop, plop* of the dots turned the tan felt on his hat to a dark khaki. His eyes lit up for a moment while he watched them land.

"Gonna be a rough one today," he mumbled to Evelyn. The tingle in his foot turned to a dull, throbbing ache. She looked up at him, her sad dog eyes trying to sympathize. She laid her head on his knee, soaking up all of his discomfort with her furry touch.

When enough rain had collected, he tipped the hat up and drank from it. The water was sweet and crisp, and only twice as cold as the air around him. He shivered as it raced through his veins. Placing his hat back on his head, he stood up slowly. Water droplets ran down his temples, softly thudding onto the collar of his jacket. Evelyn rose, took two steps ahead to give him room, and patiently waited for her master.

"Good girl."

He leaned on his good leg, the muscles in his thighs straining to support his weight from this position. He knew better than to sit anywhere that low, especially with the weather how it was. He'd have to take half a bottle of pain reliever when he got back to the ranch.

The black and white border collie stopped and looked back at him, her ears slightly cocked. *Hurry up, Dad.*

"I know, I know. Don't keep remindin' me. I didn't forget."

The steers in the field carried on about their business of chewing grass, ignoring their owner and his trusty sidekick. Elijah securely locked the gate behind him, and then hobbled over to the farther-away-than-it-should-be passenger side of his pickup truck. Evelyn patiently waited for him to open the door for her, before hopping up and taking her rightful place as shotgun.

The rain was coming down in sheets as Elijah started up the truck. With a few sputters and then a roar from the engine, the old pickup came to life. *I should probably get rid of it*, he thought to himself. *Or at least trade it in for scrap metal, and maybe get some semblance of a down payment for its bones.*

But this was the first and only truck he'd ever had, and he hated to be disloyal. Pop had picked the previously owned blue Chevy out for him on his sixteenth birthday, and emotion caught in Elijah's throat thinking how happy the old man had been when he'd presented it to him.

He shook the thought away. He wasn't much for emotional outbursts, now or ever. He glanced over at Evelyn, whose tail was thumping in a steady rhythm against the seat, giving off a sound like boots pacing a dirt floor. She knew exactly where they were headed.

It was Wednesday.

And Wednesday was Town Day.

Chapter One

"All right, so I got two stacks of flapjacks, two sides of eggs, sunny side up, and two Texas Sunrises. Anything else?" The customers shook their heads and handed Bea their menus.

"I'm on it, Toots!" Rhonda shouted across the diner, when she saw Bea holding up two fingers. Texas Sunrise was the drink of the month at Rhonda's Diner, and the locals and tourists were flocking in droves to try it.

It was only her third day at the diner, and already, Rhonda was talking about making her full-time.

"I'll only be here for the summer, before I go back to college," Bea replied to Rhonda's random outbursts of thought.

"Get on over here, I gotta teach you how to make these. I need some backup in the trenches!" Rhonda shouted. "I'm never gonna get the red out of my fingers after this."

Bea sidled up beside Rhonda as she pulled the cherry syrup from the container with her syringe. "Ain't gonna be no Texas sun risin' today, with those clouds lookin' the way they are. I'll tell ya that right now. Pay attention, this is the secret. You payin' attention?"

"Yes, ma'am," Bea said, grinning.

"All right, you hold the syringe real close to the glass, and then you shoot it real delicate, like you don't wanna hurt nobody's feelings. That way, the cherry settles in on top of the orange juice real nice and quiet, and won't blend into it.

"Oh, but first you gotta pour a half shot of Grand Marnier in the bottom. That's the secret. There's a lot of secrets. Just enough to give it a punch, but not enough to get Benjamin Matthew mad at me for juicin' people up. Not that I would ever get mad if he put me in handcuffs, know what I'm sayin'?" Her heavy accent lingered on her tongue. *Know whut Ah'm sayin'?*

She wiggled her eyebrows overdramatically, and elbowed Bea hard in the ribs. Bea winced, and tried to smile through her grimace. "When does the fruit go on?"

"That's the very last step. You gotta put a twist of an orange over the side, and three cherries on one of them little swords. People love the little swords. And I pop a sprig of mint just for some color. All right, now go, go, go!" She pushed a line of glasses towards Bea in rapid succession, and Bea delicately loaded up her tray, trying not to blend the juices too much.

She made her way around the diner, placing the drinks on practically every table that had anybody at it. As she sat the last drink down at the last table, the doorbell chimed.

Instinctively, Bea's eyes traveled towards the customer as he stepped through the door, and she nearly dropped the drink she was holding.

The thunder cracked around him as the door closed, the bell dinging at his arrival once more. He was tall, stunning, and soaked to the bone. Cowboy boots, dark jeans, and a green plaid shirt were hidden beneath a floor-length tan trench coat. The tendrils of his long, sandy-blonde hair, darkened from the storm, swirled down his shoulders like dozens of tiny tornadoes that dripped with water.

The brim of the tan cowboy hat raised slightly, and he surveyed his surroundings before choosing a seat.

His hazel eyes met with Bea's for a split second before looking through her to the vacant seat in the corner. He walked past her, and she noticed a slight limp in his step.

Bea made her way back around the counter, dropping her tray and gripping the sink for support.

Rhonda looked at her curiously. "What's wrong with you, hon?"

"I … My heart's just gone and palpitated out of my chest. Every romantic novel I've ever read just came to life and walked through the door."

Rhonda slammed down the ice cream scooper she was holding and leaned on the counter towards Bea with her elbows cradling her head. *"Gracious. Tell. Me. Everything.* Where is he? I gotta see this man."

"Back corner, cowboy hat," Bea whispered, nodding backwards with her head. She was afraid if she turned around, he'd pierce her soul and she'd pee herself. "I have never wanted a man as bad as I want him. I want him like I want grilled mushrooms and onions on top of my sirloin."

Rhonda licked her lips. "Is it wrong that I totally understand your analogy?" She looked past Bea to the corner.

"Heavens no, girl. You don't want that one. That's Elijah Callahan. Rumor has it he's a murderer."

"He's no murderer. Look at him. There's not a bad cell in that man."

"I think that's what they said about Ted Bundy, too."

"He's obviously not Ted Bundy. Misunderstood, maybe, but he's not a murderer. I wouldn't fall in love with a murderer."

"Oh, honey, I just dribbled a little bit!" Rhonda laughed as she slapped the counter. "I gotta remember to start wearin' my pantyliners again if I'm gonna keep you around. Ten minutes ago, you were here on college break, now you're in love. Goodwater Ranch certainly is a magical place!"

Bea gave herself permission to slowly turn around and look at the sparkling majesty in the corner. His head was down, examining the menu.

"He always orders the same thing; I don't know why he gets a menu. Good luck with that one, honey. He's as broody and mysterious as they come. They say he murdered Old Man Callahan. The only people who know for sure are Elijah, the old man, and Ben."

"Wait, who's Ben? I thought you said his name was Benjamin Matthew?"

"Only when I'm mad at him. Don't tell Jerry, but I'd donate my left tit to science to marry that man, even if I am old enough to be his mama. He and Elijah have been BFFs since they were in diapers. Nowadays, Benjamin Matthew Camden is the local police. Rumor has it he went into law enforcement to try and persecute Elijah because he knows the truth about that night."

"But they're still friends?"

"As far as I know of, the best."

"Then I guess he's not trying to put him away. Further proof that *Elijah* isn't a murderer." Bea loved the way his name sounded on her tongue. She silently repeated it as her boss carried on.

Rhonda waved her hand in the air dismissively. "All's I'm sayin' is, he's weird. He sits up there on his haunted ranch all day, with all his cows and chickens and horses. You know how different those chicken people can be. They've got chicken cruises!

Can you imagine? A cruise full of chicken people! Sounds like a nightmare to me. I'd rather be caught in a funhouse full of clowns." *Ah'd ratha be cawht inna funhaus fulla clouwns.*

"His house is haunted?"

"No, his whole *land* is haunted. Because he's a murderer. You've got your work cut out for you, that's for dang sure."

Bea smoothed her apron down and tightened her ponytail. She lowered her head and raised her arm ever so slightly outward, trying to casually, but not obviously, smell her armpits. *Deodorant still holding strong. Check.* "How do I look?"

"Like a million bucks, babe. Best of luck to ya!"

Bea spun on her heel, and then spun right back around. "Crap. What do I say?"

"Hmmm," Rhonda tapped her ink pen on her temple while she contemplated. "How about, 'May I take your order?' That one's free, the next line'll cost ya. I'll add a tab to your paycheck." She winked, and Bea giggled with relief. But, as soon as Bea turned back around, the tension in her throat was back.

Men had always approached Bea. She had never

been the one to do the approaching. But when she set her sights on something, she got it, and Elijah Callahan was going to be hers.

Bea took a deep breath, trying to force her nerves away. Her white Keds caught on the black and white tile floor as she exited from behind the counter. She stumbled and bounced awkwardly, trying not to face plant in front of her future husband. *Get it together, Bea.*

As she walked to his table, her vision tunneled towards him. Everyone and everything melted out of sight, and Bea decided right then and there that she wanted blue hydrangeas in her bridal bouquet.

The cowboy hat didn't move a centimeter when she stopped at his table.

"Cuuuuaaann," her throat growled in a froggy throat voice, betraying Bea's nerves and her confidence in one blow. All of the blood in her body rushed to her cheeks, making her the same color as the diner's ruby glittered seats. She quickly cleared her throat. "I mean, can I take your order?"

Elijah didn't flinch. Either he didn't notice, or he didn't care. Bea couldn't decide which was worse. She'd halfway expected him to have already pulled an engagement ring out of his pocket.

"Chicken fried steak. Mashed potatoes. Extra gravy. Sweet tea." He stated his order simply and slowly, as if she couldn't understand him. "Halfway through, two plain hamburgers to go."

"Right, coming up." Bea lingered beside the table a moment longer, admiring the view. She bit down on the tip of her ink pen, and felt something pop inside her mouth. Mortified, she prayed for it to not be the ink cartridge spurting out black ink between her lips. She turned and ran back behind the counter, and ducked down beside Rhonda.

"Mercy, girl. What's wrong now?"

Bea peered up sheepishly. "Please tell me I don't look like I just ate a bag of topsoil!"

Rhonda licked her thumb and grabbed a napkin. "I think you just popped the clicker off. But you do have a little dot here. How'd you manage to stab yourself in the mouth with the writing end?"

Bea covered her face with her palms and groaned.

"Hold still, I think I can rub it into a mole. Tomorrow it'll be gone. So, how'd it go? Are you pregnant yet?" She stood up and admired her work.

"Just like Marilyn Monroe." Rhonda ripped the ticket off and stuck it under the clip. She spun the order wheel around to her husband, who also doubled as the grill cook. "Jerry, Mr. Callahan will have his usual."

Bea stood back up, peering at her face in the reflection of the counter's chrome surface. "Thank you, Rhonda."

"Don't mention it. Hey, Jerry," she called through the window. "Let's give Mr. Callahan *the Lover's Special*, all right?"

From his position at the grill, Jerry looked around and winked at Rhonda before blowing her a kiss.

"What's the Lover's Special?" Bea asked, not wanting to humiliate herself further.

"Darlin', everybody knows the quickest way to a man's heart is through his stomach. Which puts you in the optimal seducing atmosphere. Back when Jerry was just a customer, and I had a tight little body and wasn't this saggy goddess of a hot mess, I'd load him up with so many sides he couldn't see straight. Literally, I'd make his blood sugar crash. He'd get so tired and sleepy from all the carbs and sugar that he had no choice but to listen to my siren's song."

She pointed through the window at Jerry. "As you can see, it worked like a charm. There's not a better grill master than you, baby!" Jerry wiggled his butt in response as he flipped the sizzling patties.

"OK, so what do I do?" Bea was curious now.

"Serial killer or not, ain't no man ever turned down extra mashed potatoes. So today, let's say Jerry made a mistake and now you gotta bring Mr. Callahan there six sides, plus gravy, instead of his regular two. He'll be passed out in no time, and his mashed potato-logged self will fall right into your arms like butter sliding off a hot knife. You're welcome. Load him up some sweet tea, too. Sweet tea is like love nectar."

About ten minutes later, six sides of mashed potatoes and gravy popped up in the window.

Bea felt foolish sitting so much down in front of Elijah that he clearly hadn't ordered.

"What's all this?" he grumbled. Not mad, but not exactly friendly, either.

"Jerry made a mistake."

"Jerry doesn't make mistakes."

"Well, maybe he's running a fever. I'll be sure to check his forehead. It's on the house, though. I can bring you a box if you'd like. It'll go really nice with those hamburgers later. You can even make waffles, if you have a waffle maker. If not, you can get one at Walmart. They're real cheap now, only like twenty bucks. No big deal. They say everything goes down in price the more people buy it, so I guess everybody has a waffle maker at home now. I used to think that was a rare commodity." Bea realized she was nervously rambling like a lunatic.

Her pupils dilated as Elijah finally looked up at her, his handsome face hidden behind the scruff of a wild cowboy. His hazel eyes narrowed, sizing her up. "You new here?"

She's cute, he thought. *Obviously scared to death, the way her hands are shaking, but cute. Really cute. Straight blonde hair, with pink-rimmed cat's eye glasses that look like she time-travelled back to the Fifties to get them. They oddly make her fit in better at the diner. She's short, but not too short. Curvy, and not too skinny. The kind of girl who orders a salad, just because she really does like the taste.*

"I'm here for the summer, between semesters at college. My grandma's lived here since forever. At least since I was born. I've visited a few times over the years, but she said the air would be a good change for me. I'm a junior at Austin. Well, technically a senior now, I suppose. I've got two semesters left before I graduate." She was rambling again, and doing her best not to stutter. He'd overheard Rhonda telling her he was a murderer, and figured that's why she was terrified.

Elijah tried his best to avoid most people on most days, which was why he came into town on Wednesdays only. Conveniently, Wednesdays at lunchtime, Rhonda was usually out getting her hair done into whatever stiff, pastel-colored beehive of a mess she was going to sport that week.

Elijah actively tried not to come in here when she was here, because she was always quick to start even more rumors. Whatever thought popped into her head at any given moment, by the next day was thought of as a town fact. Jerry was nicer, quieter, and had a lot more common sense. For the life of him, Elijah couldn't figure out why a man like Jerry would ever have fallen in love with a noise clacker like Rhonda.

By the time he'd seen Rhonda, he was already inside. It would've made people talk even more if he'd turned around and left, so he kept his head down and sat in the corner, away from Rhonda's line of sight. He'd just as much prefer to go over to The Avocado Taco to get a bite, but he would've had to come here for the burgers anyway. Evelyn didn't really care for Tex-Mex.

"Who's your grandma?" Elijah had to know what level of psycho was handling his food, and he couldn't remember if Rhonda had ever had kids or not.

"Millie. Millie St. Claire. Do you know her? She's the local florist."

Elijah felt some of the tension let out of his chest. Millie was on his list of sane and preferable people. And she hated Rhonda even more than he did, which didn't add up because then why was the girl working here?

"What's your name?" he asked, ignoring her question. He wasn't sure why he was still asking her questions, either, except to solve the mystery in his head of how six servings of potatoes had landed on his table.

"Bea," she squeaked.

"Like bumble?" He finished off one of the eight glasses of sweet tea she'd placed in front of him in the last ten minutes since he'd ordered.

She bit her lip to suppress her cheesy grin, as if he were the most hilarious person on earth. "Like Albuquerque."

"You're in the wrong city and state, Albuquerque. There's no Bea in that."

"Yeah, well, my family used to call me Albie, and over the years it got shortened to Bea. Better than what the kids in grade school called me, which was Quirky. Imagine that. 'What's up, AlbuQuirky?' It haunted me for years. But now I like it because nobody else has it."

"You got a couple of empty gallon jugs?"

"What?"

"For this tea. Hate to dump it down the drain. Can't drink five gallons in one sitting."

She slapped the air in front of her and cocked her hip out to the side, as if he'd just cracked the best joke ever. "I'll see what I can find." She whipped her head as she laughed, and her ponytail came back around and smacked her face.

Bea looked at him stunned, then spun on her heel and scampered back behind the counter to Rhonda's protection. A few minutes later, she returned with yet another glass of sweet tea, the two hamburgers, and the check. She also had a to-go box and an empty plastic maraschino cherry jug.

"This was all I could find. But I washed it out for you. It'll be fine. And if not, cherry tea might be the next drink of the month! You never know what'll catch on. Like, I still can't believe there are pickle-flavored potato chips. Who knew that was going to be a thing?"

Elijah dumped the tea into the jug, and screwed the lid on tightly. Then he quickly slid the five sides on potatoes into the box. Normally, he'd take his time eating, but today he was ready to go home as fast as he could. He took money out of his wallet, more than enough to cover the food plus a nice tip for Bea for her over-service.

All while she stood there, watching him with her mouth hanging open.

Elijah didn't think he was that much of a sideshow, but he noticed Rhonda watching him now, too. Suddenly, he felt like he was in a fishbowl. He quickly slid out of the booth, ignoring the throbbing pain in his leg.

"Say hello to your grandmother for me," was all he could think to say as he hobbled out of the diner as fast as he could.

Bea ran behind the counter and promptly sank to the floor. "I. Am. Completely. Mortified." She covered her face with her hands and wadded herself up in a ball in the corner.

Chapter Two

"Do you think he's a murderer?" Bea asked her grandma while she washed the dishes. "Rhonda said—"

"Oh, pish on Rhonda. That woman is crazier than a June bug hopped up on speed. The only thing she knows about is food. Anything else she says is complete and utter nonsense, and likely beyond her mental capabilities." Millie pointed her finger at Bea. "And don't you let her fool you otherwise. There's a lot of bad history mixed in with the good, and a lot of bad spirits that haunt the mountains. But none of that has anything to do with Elijah. That boy is one of the gentlest souls I know. He wouldn't pour salt on a slug. He would rather talk to animals than people, because he knows they won't disappoint him. Most of the rumors about him were perpetrated by none other than Rhonda and her posse of putrid pickaninnies."

"How old is this 'boy'? He can't be over thirty. I'm twenty-two. That's not bad." She put the plates away, just as the scent of casserole hit her nostrils. "I think the food is almost done."

Millie pulled the chicken tetrazzini out of the oven, her glasses immediately steaming up. The olive-y, creamy smells of goodness washed over Bea and all the happy memories from staying with her grandma when she was a young girl came rushing back to her. Rhonda was *not* a better cook than Millie, not according to Bea, at least.

"Well, let's see." Millie removed her glasses to rub the steam off with her shirt. "I'm sixty-eight. I think, I want to say, he's about twenty-five. Maybe twenty-eight." She waved her hands in the air dismissively. "Somewhere between there. The years start slipping away so fast, and you can't catch them. Then, one day you're just standing there counting, and you realize you lost ten or so somewhere, maybe scattered in the junk drawer of life."

Bea was smiling to herself. He was younger than she thought, even though he looked a little rough around the edges.

"Why are you so curious about Elijah?" Millie asked, as she put her glasses on, clearly seeing Bea's lovesick expression for the first time.

"Because I'm going to marry him." Her heart fluttered even as she said it, and her skin got all tingly.

"Well, Bea-utiful," her grandma always called her, "you picked a tough nut to crack. That one's more reserved that a dilapidated restaurant. He's always been a total muffin to me, even done some yard work for me here and there. But you know how little towns are. Family curses, ghosts in the wind, all that sort of nonsense."

"Is that why he limps? I noticed that today. He said to tell you hello, by the way."

Millie paused and looked at a spot on the wall, trying to remember. "It started after Old Man Callahan died. Elijah would never talk about it, though. Not to me at least. They say the Callahan mine is haunted, so it could be a ghost that's dragging him down." She lowered her head, peering over her glasses at Bea. "You already talked to him? You've only been here since Saturday."

"Yeah, he came in the diner today at lunch. He's awful young to have so many legends and stories about him already. Especially for someone who doesn't talk that much." Bea grabbed a trivet and sat the casserole on the center of the table. Next, she got out two salad bowls and the homemade ranch dressing that only Millie could ever make perfectly.

"Maybe that's why. The more mysterious he is, the more people make up stories. Legends are like dead leaves—one swift breeze and before you know it, they're piling up everywhere around you. He usually keeps to himself, so if he's talking to you, I'd say you're on the right track." She patted Bea on her shoulder as they sat down at the table to eat.

"I don't think I made a great impression. He made me so nervous. I've never been that nervous around anybody before, but he was just so … so … *pretty*."

"He is a cutie, that's for sure. I bet he's got a really tight butt, too."

"Grammy!" Bea was mid-drink and nearly choked on an ice cube as she slammed her glass back down on the table.

"Oh, sure, because you didn't notice *anything* besides his eyeballs. I know better than that, you're my flesh and blood after all. He's up there all alone, all day, just mining, chasing cows and riding horses. He's got nothing to do but stay in shape."

Bea ate her tetrazzini, silently contemplating her

next move. Her grandma was two steps ahead of her. Millie smiled, a knowing look passing behind her glasses.

"You're a St. Claire, Bea. What would a St. Claire do?"

"Push back until you push through." That's what her parents always taught her. Her dad said it was basically their family motto. Anytime any adversity faced them, they pushed back until they pushed through.

"Sounds like a good plan to me. As good a plan as any."

~

Bea didn't sleep the whole night. Her mind raced and wandered, thought and pondered, until she came up with a plan so brilliant, it couldn't possibly fail.

The next morning, she bounded into the kitchen. Millie was frying bologna on homemade biscuits.

"Well, what's the verdict?"

"I'm going to ask if I can sketch him."

Millie sliced two biscuits open, and laid fried eggs

and fried bologna inside, before sliding a pat of butter on top and closing up her masterpiece. "It's a start. What's your reasoning?"

"I'm an art student. I'm here for the summer. I'm working on my portfolio. What's better than a portrait of a real live cowboy on a real live ranch? It's a creative inspiration minefield."

"Sounds good to me." Millie bit into her biscuit, the butter dripping down her fingers as she did so. "How're you going to do it?"

"I'm going to walk right up to him and ask if I can draw him."

"How's about you take some of last night's tetrazzini to soften the blow? He's a reclusive man. He keeps to himself and doesn't care much for human interaction, so you've got that working against you. Plus, men are like cockroaches—as soon as they see you pointing a light at them, they run and hide in the corners.

"What I'm saying is, it's going to be an uphill battle for you, all the way. But he's a good man, and you're my granddaughter. Quite frankly, I'm excited to see how this is going to play out. Go get your man, Bea!"

Chapter Three

Bea had the day off from the diner, so she took extra care to make herself look as adorable as possible. She left her corn silk hair down, falling around her shoulders, and swept her bangs to the side. She applied light make-up, not too heavy, but certainly a bit of darkened eyeshadow and lipstick to make her look more mature.

Next, she chose a light blue sundress. Bea twirled in the mirror and frowned, realizing she looked more like a gothic Alice than like a woman who was about to land the man of her dreams.

Back into her suitcases she went, until a yellow T-shirt and blue denim jeans called her name. Bea paired them with the only pair of cowboy boots she had, a nice beige pair with black stitching, that looked more chic than practical. She wondered to herself how a nice summer with her grandma had turned into a mission to land a husband, and then frowned at herself again for not doing better to forward the feminist movement along.

But dang, if they'd have seen him, they'd understand.

Bea grabbed the bag out of the refrigerator, containing the tetrazzini and some slices of garlic bread Millie had carefully rolled in aluminum foil, along with the hand-drawn map of how to get to Elijah's.

If there was one thing Bea was certain of, now more than yesterday, it was that Elijah Callahan was not a murderer. If he was, there was no way on God's green earth that Millie St. Claire would be allowing him anywhere near her prized chicken tetrazzini.

Bea started her silver Toyota Yaris and headed out of the yard, down the gravel driveway that wound between Millie's flowerbeds and fields of silver dollar Lunaria that were growing wild. Their translucent blooms, if you could call them blooms, had always mystified Bea. When she was little, Millie had told her they were fairy trampolines. Fairies were able to fly around her gardens because they weren't really flying at all, she'd said. They were just bouncing from one money plant to another.

Bea turned and headed down the highway for several miles, admiring all of Goodwater's peculiarities. For whatever reason, she noticed a lot of people had bags of water taped to their screen doors. And more than a few had chicken wire strung up around their mailbox posts, keeping the mailbox at a safe distance from whatever mailboxes needed protecting from. Bea made a mental note to ask her grandma about those later.

When she got to the town square, traffic was rerouted. There were several policemen standing out in the street, trying their best to direct the traffic and crowds at the same time. Bea slowly drove around the town square, trying to chance a peek at the movie that was currently filming.

Most of the congestion of the traffic was due to the amount of people who regularly showed up to try and get their big shot on-screen in the background. Before yesterday happened, Bea had planned on going and hanging out on all the sets on her off days, hoping to get picked to become an extra.

Not today, Bea thought. *I'll be a movie star some other day.*

She continued up the highway, past the historical society that was the original Goodwater Ranch, continuing on until the trees replaced the houses, and the mountains replaced the buildings. The wonderful thing about Goodwater Ranch was that there was something for everyone, which was why people were so drawn to it.

Want to be on a movie set? Check the calendar, or buy a local paper to see what's filming currently.

Want to go to a Fall Festival, a Boot Sale, or a Barn Raising? You've come to the right place!

Want to get your jams, jellies, pies, and jerkies judged in the county fair, or try your shot at winning the annual Halloween costume contest? May the best win!

Do you like mountain climbing, fly fishing, rodeos, and rock climbing? Goodwater Ranch has excellent recreational activities for those of you who are more adventurous!

Professional sports more your cup of tea? Over on the west side, on the border between Goodwater Ranch and Eagle's Nest, are where the stadium and the arena are located. We've got the NFL's Goodwater Gold Diggers, and the NHL's Knickabrick Knockarounds, sure to keep you entertained!

When her parents were convincing Bea to spend the summer with her grandmother, they didn't have to convince her too hard. It wasn't that she didn't want to be here, per se.

It was that she could've been drawing the Eiffel Tower in Paris instead, if she'd had enough funds. Neither she nor her parents had enough money for Bea to go on the college semester trip abroad.

Initially, it had been a bummer. Bea had always dreamed of backpacking through Europe, living some exotic foreign adventure like they do in the movies. Even with trying to pool her savings together with what her parents had, she wasn't anywhere close to the twelve-thousand dollars she would've needed for the three-month-long excursion.

But now.

All that was before she knew Elijah Callahan existed. As of yesterday, Bea didn't feel quite as cheated by life anymore. In fact, she now felt she had been put in the right place at the right time.

She turned left when the roads diverged, on the path less taken. The clouds rolled overhead and settled on top of the mountains, signaling there would be another storm in the not-too-distant future. The clouds cast a darkened mood over the landscape, and as Bea glanced out at her surroundings, she couldn't help but feel the sense of mystery and intrigue grow.

Far in the distance, there were fields with steers, their brown bodies standing out against the shadows and grass. Behind the field, off in the distance, there was a dark hole. Millie, or Rhonda, she couldn't remember which, had said there was an old mine up here. Another possible clue to the legends that surrounded the Callahan place.

If Bea had been a gambler, she'd have bet a dollar it was haunted as well. Mentally, she added "ghost hunting" to her ever-growing checklist of things to accomplish this summer.

The road twisted until it ended at an overgrown gravel path that headed right, towards the direction of the mine. Bea turned, her car tires crunching against the ground as she rolled slowly through the trees. Overgrown was more of an understatement. Downright forgotten was more accurate. If ever a haunted forest existed, this was it. Fog settled low on the ground, while old, hanging limbs sprawled overhead, attached only by kudzu, to trees that may, or may not still be alive. Bea couldn't decide if the trees had just given up for the summer, or if they were truly, deeply dead.

Finally, her car emerged from the Forest of Decay into a clearing that wasn't much better. Junk littered the yard; old car parts and old pieces of furniture had been haphazardly strewn up into piles, like somebody had started a bonfire fifty years ago but had forgotten to light it.

The house wasn't much better. Elijah's great-grandpa had built the house back in the 1940s, and it had been a family heirloom of sorts, passed down through four generations. It had been beautiful in its time, a two-storied farmhouse with a wrap-around porch and bay windows running up one side.

In its current state, it looked as run-down as the rest of the surroundings. Bea got out of her car and carefully trod up to the porch. She stopped at the base of the stairs, admiring the catastrophe around her. The wood of it wasn't rotten, yet, but it was extremely weathered—dark gray and green from age, with splintered paint curling up at the ends of each of the boards.

"What in the heck ..." Bea whispered to herself. *Nobody can live like this*, she thought. *Why would anybody live like this?* She hadn't been expecting her prince to really live in a castle, but she had expected him to at

least take the trash out. She struggled to recall the part of any of the fairy tales where the princess had to clean out her own castle first before living happily ever after.

The old screen door whipped open, smacking against the side of the house. At the sound of her car crunching to a halt, Elijah stepped out and Bea's heart stopped. He looked even better than he had yesterday. Cowboy boots, tight jeans, and an even tighter navy blue, V-neck T-shirt did nothing to disguise Bea's fantasies of what lay underneath. His dark blond hair was down, hanging well past his shoulders in a wild and unruly lion's mane.

A black and white border collie bounded out from behind him. She ran up to Bea and started licking her knees in a welcoming gesture. Bea leaned down to pet her, and the dog stuck her nose into the bag and wagged her tail. Elijah propped one shoulder against one of the wooden columns of the porch and crossed his arms.

"You lost? The movie set isn't up here."

"I thought we got off on the wrong foot is all." Bea nervously shifted her weight from side to side.

"What foot would that be?" He stared at her,

awaiting her brilliant retort.

Push back until you push through, a voice in her head reminded her. Bea stood up a little straighter, and remembered why she was here. Her wallflower self wasn't getting anything accomplished this way. It was time to fake it till she made it.

The dog bit the side of the bag, bringing Bea back to reality. She looked down as the garlic bread rolled out of the aluminum and onto the ground. The dog looked up at Bea, surprised that she'd accomplished such a feat. Then, the dog looked up at Elijah for permission to enjoy her spoils of war. He nodded at her, before shifting his gaze back to Bea.

"I guess I brought that for her, then," Bea said lightly, trying to make him smile. He didn't.

"Well, anyway. You said tell my grandmother hello, so I did. She said she hadn't seen you in a while and that I should bring you this, because you don't have a woman to take care of you. So, that's what I'm going to do."

Bea looked around the landscape, shaking her head disapprovingly. "It looks like I've got my work cut out for me." She marched up the stairs and past Elijah, straight into the house, stopping halfway in between the foyer and who-knows-where. "Can you show me where the kitchen is? I'll heat this up for you and then start cleaning."

"I don't need a maid." Elijah said begrudgingly, turning around to look at this short woman who'd just walked into his home uninvited.

"That's exactly what you *do* need. Look at this place! It used to be beautiful, I can tell. I don't know what happened, but I've got two months to get it turned around." The dog walked in and sat beside her, in a show of support. Bea leaned down to scratch her ears. "Isn't that right, girl? What might your name be?"

"Used to be Evelyn. I changed it to Traitor just today."

She looked up at him, searching his handsomeness for any trace of a smile at the joke he had just cracked. "Ah, so there is a personality in there somewhere. Maybe more of it will come out when you get some of Millie's famous tetrazzini inside you." And with that, Bea stood up and stomped through the house in search of the oven.

Evelyn and Elijah followed her in close pursuit. "I'm not paying you."

"I don't remember asking you to. A man shouldn't have to do everything on his own. You need some help around here. I'm here to help you. Be grateful for the gifts life gives you."

Elijah huffed under his breath, but Bea just ignored him. She found the kitchen on her own, wading through the stacks of newspapers and dirty dishes to find the oven.

Bea looked around in disbelief. It was an old kitchen, and everything except the microwave and the stove appeared to be original to the home. Wallpaper was peeling from the walls, the linoleum was peeling from the floor, and there were more cobwebs than crystals in the crystal chandelier that hung over the dining room table, that was also piled with junk for the ages.

She waved her arms around frantically. "This! All this! This whole room is a fire hazard. What on earth is going on here?" The stovetop, at least, was cleaned off except for a dirty pan that looked like it'd only held beans or some sort of contraption. She turned it on, and somehow managed to scrounge up a clean pan from the depths of despair.

"I don't *owe* you an explanation for marching into my home, *girl*," Elijah growled as he stood in the doorway, blocking the escape that he anticipated Bea trying to make. She did not. She turned around slowly, like a cat creeping up on a bird. Not much pissed Bea off more, or quicker, than being treated like a child.

"Look here, *boy*. You haven't asked me to leave yet, either." Elijah's body didn't flinch, but his pupils grew wide in shock at her shift in dominance. Bea took that as a sign to continue. "I did my research before I came here. You're only a few years older than me. Do. Not. Ever. call me 'girl' again. Now sit your ass down in that chair while I cook you lunch. Unless you'd like to help me wash these dishes, that is. Otherwise, I'd advise you to take some notes on how it's done."

Elijah's Adam's apple bobbed as he swallowed. It was barely visible beneath his beard, but just evident enough for Bea to feel like she'd won this silent battle. She narrowed her eyes at him, further daring him to try and cross her. She was obviously not afraid of him, murderer or not.

Elijah walked over to the chair, his limp slightly better today after the pain relievers had kicked in.

"What happened to your foot?" Bea asked, her voice changing back to polite now that she was satisfied with his obedience to her. She opened and closed all of the cabinet doors looking for dish soap while she waited for an answer. During her search, she found an entire roll of garbage bags and decided to start with those, though she'd make a note to get all the cleaning supplies she needed before coming back.

"What happened to your glasses?" Elijah countered. Bea stopped and turned to face him. *Had he noticed more about me than I'd thought, or even dared to dream?* She felt her heart race as she tried not to overreact.

"You noticed my glasses?" she asked, focusing on keeping her voice as steady as possible.

"Hard not to notice. Looked like you'd gotten lost on your way to a *Grease* revival."

Bea put her hands on her hips and enunciated with a sugary-sweet Southern drawl, "Well, I do declare! Elijah Callahan knows what *Grease* is? I have never, in all my wildest days!"

He watched her work, in equal parts shock and awe at her feistiness. The girl who was scared of him yesterday was nowhere to be seen. The girl, *woman*, he corrected himself, who'd replaced her was moving around the kitchen and making a home for herself right before his eyes. By the time the tetrazzini had heated up, she'd already pulled out everything from the cabinets and made nice, neatly organized piles on the floors.

Bea washed a dinner plate, and piled it high with the tetrazzini. The last time he'd had an honest-to-goodness home-cooked meal was … *was* … Well, he couldn't remember right off, but he wasn't going to think too hard about it.

The steam from the food rose, and Elijah couldn't tell if it was burning his eyes, or if his eyes stung from tears. Millie's tetrazzini was a prize winner, and an elusive unicorn as far as town legends went. It was something everyone knew about, but only a lucky few had had.

No. He was definitely *not* crying over tetrazzini. It was the steam. It was extra steamy, for whatever reason. Bea continued to keep herself occupied with cleaning while he ate, thank goodness. He glanced over at the stove, checking to see if maybe there was enough for seconds. There was, but Bea saw him looking and beat him to it.

"I got it. You sit back down." Elijah promptly sat back down and let Bea serve him for the second time that day.

"OK, here's the plan. I'm going to go to the Dollar Club to get everything I need. When I come back, the gloves are off. Technically on, but you know what I mean. And you better not lock me out of this house, or I *will* break a window to get back in. I'm starting with the kitchen, whether you like it or not."

Elijah looked at her looking at him. Something, somewhere, crackled in his heart. He didn't know what it was, but he knew he didn't like it.

"I'm still not paying you. And I'm not paying for cleaning supplies."

"I still didn't ask you to. And I'm not asking your permission, either." Bea moved to leave, but stopped when she got to the doorway of the kitchen. "If you're still here in about two hours, I'll need to borrow your truck. You can help me with hauling stuff away. If you're not here, I'll assume you're doing cow stuff and we can do it tomorrow instead."

Elijah sat at the kitchen table, listening. Her boots thudded through the house, making contact with the old wooden flooring. The screen door opened and then slammed shut, as the boots clomped down the stairs and finally disappeared.

He looked down into Evelyn's big brown eyes. Her tail thumped once, like she was afraid to let him know that she'd made a new friend. Then, he looked around the kitchen and dining room at the piles and trails Bea had made for herself.

Chapter Four

When Bea arrived back at the Callahan house, Elijah's blue truck was nowhere to be seen. She grumbled to herself loudly, already frustrated at how her love story was playing out so far. This messy, sexy conundrum of a man was not conforming to her meet-cute standards very well. But he obviously did need her help, whether he wanted to admit it or not. The house and property looked like a family of hoarders had moved in during the 1800s and never moved out. If they had moved out, how would anyone know?

Bea pulled on her heavy-duty rubber gloves and got down on her hands and knees. She'd bought a can of bug spray to keep with her, which was now holstered into the belt loop of her shorts, just in case there were spiders and Elijah didn't happen to be around to save her. She started wiping out the bottom cabinets with cleaning supplies and rags, one section at a time.

She continued with her tasks, carefully lining the

bottoms of the cabinets with a white-marbled contact paper, to attract light and make it easier to keep them organized in the future.

When she was satisfied with her progress on that, Bea then grabbed a roll of garbage bags and started cleaning up all of the random trash and mess. She knew men were messy, from how her roommate back in the dorms complained about her boyfriend all the time. But *this?* This beat all she ever could've imagined.

Bea thought, trying to understand what would've made Elijah be such a slob. He was a well-dressed, physically chiseled perfection of a man. And he was obviously *not* lazy, because he ran this farm/ranch/mine—whatever it was, she didn't know the differences—by himself as far as she was aware of.

She heard Evelyn bark in the distance, somewhere outside. Bea stood up and brushed herself off, trying to be a somewhat presentable version of the Bea who'd shown up … six hours ago? She looked at her phone. Time had completely slipped away from her somehow. But then again, when Bea got focused on something, there was no turning back.

She glanced out the kitchen window, admiring the

pinks and oranges of the setting sun, which were swirling above the craggy mountain line. The screen door slammed shut, the creak of its hinges not even bothering to brace the wooden exterior of the door from slapping against its frame.

The house was darkened now, the only light coming from the kitchen, where Bea had been working. Evelyn's light paws ran up the stairs as fast as they could carry her, oblivious to her new friend. Bea listened, hanging on a breath at the sound of Elijah's footsteps as he realized she was still inside. The heavy thud of his boots moved from the front door to the stairway, stopped, and instead headed down towards the kitchen.

Bea watched the ground as the steps slowed, and the gentle *clip-clop* of his gait as he accommodated for his limp. A small puff of dust accompanied him, and Bea made a mental note to bring a broom and vacuum tomorrow. The floor was going to be a whole other chore.

Elijah stood in the doorway, almost completely filling it, and gently propped his shoulder against the frame. Bea's eyes traveled up, up, up Elijah's tall body until she met his gaze. He was staring at her intently, and her breath caught in her throat.

"You're still here," he said, emotionless. His eyes shifted around the room, sizing up what she'd done. There were at least ten trash bags piled up against the wall, tied and nearly bursting at the seams to contain their contents. The counter was slightly organized, though Bea still had a lot to do before she could be truly satisfied with her progress.

"And you weren't," she said. Though she hadn't been invited or allowed, technically, to do any of the things she'd done today, Bea wasn't going to let him run over her, either. "What do you do all day?"

"Cow stuff," he said, mocking her earlier assumption. Just for a fraction of a second, Bea caught a devious glimmer in his expression.

The silence between them was deafening. Elijah watched her like he was stalking prey while she stood there, uncomfortably seen like a fly in a web. Bea turned around, mindlessly scrubbing the counters with her cloth, just to have something to do with her hands.

"Aren't you scared?" he finally asked, slightly shifting in the doorway to resituate his weight onto his good foot.

"I was, but that's why I got the heavy-duty Super

Zapper here." Bea pulled the bug spray from her belt loop holster and twirled it around her finger like a cowboy in an old Western movie. "They scattered like marbles when they saw me coming." She blew on the nozzle end.

"No. Of me." He raised his head slightly, as if challenging her. In actuality, this only gave Bea a better view of his face, or at least as much as she could see behind his beard. She felt her cheeks flush, just as the sound of Evelyn's toenails scratched somewhere above them on the second floor.

They both stood there in the quiet house, listening to the dog's soft feet click across the wooden floorboards. It seemed she had realized her master wasn't doing his usual routine, and she had decided to investigate. Her dog feet clambered loudly down the old wooden stairs and headed towards the kitchen.

Evelyn's head wrapped around Elijah's leg, looking up at him in admiration, before realizing they still had company. She pushed past him and immediately went to sit beside Bea.

Bea leaned down to pet her head, and she could've sworn that Evelyn was smiling. If that's a thing dogs even do.

"No. Why would I be afraid of you, Elijah?" Bea had heard somewhere that using people's names in conversation was a good way to connect. Plus, she liked how his name felt on her tongue, filled with sweetness like a drop from a honeysuckle blossom.

"Because of what they say."

"People *say* lots of things just to hear themselves talk. I *feel* lots of things. But fear isn't anywhere on the list of emotions I feel for you, Elijah." She reached down and scratched behind Evelyn's ears again. "Besides, no murderer I've ever heard of gets his dog hamburgers from a restaurant on a routine basis." Bea felt her cheeks blush. In her own weird, twisted way, she'd all but told him she was in love with him already. Elijah continued to stand there in the doorway, watching her.

"Right, then. I suppose it's too late to run all this to the landfill, so we can do it later. I've got to get going because I'm working the breakfast shift, but I'll be back tomorrow afternoon. See you then?"

He nodded slightly, and still Bea couldn't read him. She marched forward towards him, and he stayed unmoving in her path.

Then, Bea did something she probably shouldn't

have done.

Taking the opportunity to touch him, with any excuse she could come up with, Bea placed her hand on his stomach as she moved to slide past him. Beneath her fingers, his hardened muscles flinched at her touch.

A rush of warmth flooded her body, and Bea let out a slight gasp that she prayed he hadn't been able to hear. She stumbled to the door as gracefully as she could, her head swimming as her reality was seriously starting to blur into her fantasies.

In her car, Bea rested her forehead against her steering wheel and sighed loudly. Facing Rhonda and her grandmother wasn't something Bea was ready for yet. She knew Elijah was hiding the majority of himself from her. But as they say, no news is good news. And there was not really any news of significance to report back.

He hadn't kicked her out, he hadn't thanked her, and he hadn't welcomed her to return. He hadn't really said much of anything.

He was just there. Unassuming, uncomplaining, unwelcoming, unreadable Elijah.

With his rock hard, rippled abs and broodiness.

Chapter Five

"Darlin', you mean you just marched into that man's home and started cleanin' up his mess? What on God's green earth was goin' through your noggin'?" Rhonda stared at Bea, bewildered by her tale.

"You should've seen it. I couldn't stop myself! I keep everything so organized, and it was just a disaster area. There's no way he lives like that, or wants to live like that! He just needs help is all. And I'm going to be the one to help him."

"Were you not listenin' to a blame thing I said the other day? The. Way. To. A. Man's. Heart. Is. Through. His. Stomach." Rhonda clapped her hands behind every word. "I did not say washing machine or trash can. S.T.O.M.A.C.H."

"Rhonda, I couldn't find it for all the clutter!"

"Oh LAWD." Rhonda fanned herself dramatically. She turned around and yelled through the window. "Jerry, this one here's gonna give me a heart attack. When it happens, you tell Dr. Halston it wasn't my

cholesterol or your cookin', it was this child right
here."

"The way I see it, is I've got eight weeks to make
an impression big enough to win that man's heart.
I'm not going to be one of those lovesick weirdos
and come back here every summer praying he'll
notice me. He's noticing me, or we're done."

"Well, darlin', at least you have *some* sort of a
boundary. You hold onto that, you're gonna need it
later. I can feel my blood pressure risin' up through
my orthopedic shoes."

~

"Do not tell that woman a single thing that you
don't want broadcast on a billboard over the whole
town. I heard about you already at the post office
today, before your shift was even over. I went to the
counter to get my package, and Missy asked me how
things were going between you and Elijah. She
wanted to know whether or not you had had an
official first date yet."

"What? Are you serious?" Bea got out lunch meat,
cheese, and mayonnaise from the fridge while they
talked.

"As the IRS. That woman is incorrigible."

Bea covered her face with her hands. "Oh, no. This is so embarrassing. Do you think Elijah knows? I feel like I'm in elementary school now!"

Millie leaned against the counter, crossing her arms as she spoke. "To his credit, that boy keeps to himself. He doesn't much talk to anyone that I know of, except Detective Camden and Darby down at the Co-op. I seriously doubt he's caught wind from anyone, unless it's already made its way over to Darby, who wouldn't give two shakes of a wet stick what was going on anyway. He's pretty good to mind his own business, unless the gossip is really juicy. How'd it go yesterday, anyway?"

"It went. I'm not sure what direction, but it went somewhere. Have you ever been to the Callahan ranch?"

"Can't say that I have. Is it nice?" Millie untied a loaf of bread and started assembling the sandwiches.

"Anything but. I'm going back after lunch. I'm going to help him clean the place up, whether he likes it or not."

Millie cut the sandwiches into quarters. "Be careful

with that. Men aren't too smart at recognizing grand gestures as a declaration of your undevoted love and admiration."

"That's what Rhonda said, too, more or less. She said the way to his heart is through his stomach, not his garbage can."

"I never thought I'd live to see the day when she and I agreed on something. Don't forget why you went out there in the first place, Bea."

"To get him to propose?" Bea shoved a sandwich square into her mouth.

Millie laughed. "No, to sketch him and his land."

Bea's eyes went wide as she tried to swallow, but the bread was stuck in the roof of her mouth. "Icom pete eek horgot!" she mumbled with her mouth full.

"Don't go putting the cart before the proverbial horse, Albuquerque." Millie was the only one who ever still called her by her full name, and that was usually out of exasperation for whatever the situation was.

Bea loaded her car up with cleaning items she'd borrowed from Millie, along with the produce boxes she'd asked Jerry to save her from that morning.

Then, not forgetting her true mission, Bea shoved her sketch pad, charcoals, and pastels into her backpack and headed out to the car. A broom and a mop stuck out of the passenger window like two chopsticks, bouncing up and down against the glass as the car rolled towards the road.

~

Elijah's driveway had already started taking on a different feel to it, after just one day. Or at least that's what it felt like to Bea. Glancing through the trees and brush, she imagined that scene from *Beauty and the Beast* when the curse is broken and all of the doom and gloom is washed away by a bright, happy future.

In actuality, the only thing that was different was that the clouds from the past week had finally blown over and the sun was shining. But Bea didn't let that dampen her mood or perception in the slightest.

Approaching the house, she noticed that the bags of garbage she'd previously left in the kitchen were now piled in the back of Elijah's truck. Bea smiled to herself, pleased with her minor accomplishment of getting him to help her.

It was quiet inside the house. Come to think of it,

Bea hadn't really been paying attention to see if Elijah even owned a television. She was used to some sort of a constant noise, even if it was just the TV playing in the background for company. The constant serenity, or isolation, that seemed to surround Elijah constantly was something Bea wasn't even close to being used to.

She heard Evelyn bark from somewhere behind the house at about the same time she noticed the back door was slightly ajar. She really liked the idiosyncratic things in Elijah's house, like how the front door opened into a hallway that led straight to the back door. She remembered, from various tours she'd gone on of old homes, how that was a common design feature to allow fresh air to filter through the entire house.

Bea headed straight back, smiling at the wooden shelf built into the wall, with a now unused phone jack. To make use of the space, Elijah's keys, cellphone, and wallet now lay there, inside a little wicker basket. So, he *could* be organized, if he really wanted to be.

She made a mental note that someday soon, when Elijah was out, she was going to prop open every door and window in this place and blast him with fresh air. This house, unfortunately, smelled more like a dirty, dusty antique store than a bachelor pad.

She propped the broom and mop up against the kitchen wall before turning to exit through the old screen door.

Four lush, sprawling maple trees greeted her, forming a makeshift path to the rest of the backyard. Right past them, she saw Evelyn chasing a chicken.

Oh, right. They're chicken people. Whatever that means.

Bea headed down through the backyard, towards the chicken coop. She noted more than several old, rusty buckets beneath the trees, along with old wooden crates. The backyard looked to be in much better shape, more loved and cared for than any other part of the house or grounds she'd seen so far. And despite the clutter around the trees, it still wasn't nearly as bad as the front yard, which looked more like a landfill.

Passing the last tree, Elijah came into full view and Bea's heart skipped at least ten beats. He was wearing tight jeans; a green, buttoned-up shirt rolled up to his elbows; with his signature tan Stetson hat and a wicker basket hooked onto his arm. And he was talking.

Bea tiptoed towards him, to try and hear what he was whispering to the chickens. Still unnoticing of her, he was leant down, nearly eye level with his feathered posse and talking more to the chickens than he'd talked to her. Ever.

And in full sentences, no less.

Chicken people.

He reached into the coop, and delicately retrieved an egg. "Look at that egg, Hannah! I think that's the most beautiful one this week."

He held it up to the chicken, so they could both lovingly gaze at its egginess. "You're a pro, Hannah! That's three today. Thank you for being so motivated." Elijah scratched the soft feathers on her neck, and as he did so, Hannah the chicken and Bea the human both lovingly stared at him in awe.

He's a chicken whisperer.

Bea's fists clenched as a twig snapped beneath her foot, alerting Elijah to her presence. With his back still to her, he stood up, immediately going silent. Other than his now, and obviously selective, muteness, he didn't acknowledge Bea otherwise.

Bea had never been so jealous of a chicken in her

entire life.

She cleared her throat, trying to break the ice she was frozen solid in. "Maple syrup trees aren't supposed to grow outside of New England."

Elijah sighed, his shoulders slightly raising and falling with the absolute knowledge that Bea had, in fact, come back for a second day. He turned slowly, his face squinting in a sarcastic expression. His eyes dragged up one side of the miniature forest, and down the other until they landed on her.

"Looks like they do."

Bea was instantly so frustrated that she wanted to scream. She mentally debated the pros and cons of throwing Hannah into a stockpot, before deciding that would set her back too far. Bea clenched her teeth together. "I see that. My point is that they shouldn't. My grandma is a florist. I have learned a thing or two over the years."

Elijah turned back away from her and continued collecting eggs. A few seconds passed between them before she heard an audible, "Good water."

"The town?"

"The reason." Elijah delicately placed the eggs, one

by one, inside the wicker basket hanging from the crook of his elbow, while his flock of feathered women cuddled at his feet. Evelyn went racing past, the same chicken she'd been chasing earlier now hot on her heels.

"They do say it's magical. I don't know how much of that I believe, though. I'm thinking of getting one of the bottled water keychains for my roommate at school. Did you know they have water-filled picture frames at the gift shop?" Bea felt herself starting to venture into rambling territory to calm her irritation, but it was either that or ring Hannah's neck, so she let herself go.

"And snow globes, of course. Whatever you can imagine, really. I don't think it's all the good water, though. I think it's probably just regular water and they're trying to make a buck. Has to be. I mean, have you ever seen someone hanging out at Tutwiler Springs filling up picture frames? It seems absurd that that would be somebody's actual job. 'What do you do for a living?' 'Fill up picture frames with magic water.'"

Elijah had turned back to face her, his eyes slowly closing and silently willing her to shut up. Bea took the hint.

"Well, anyway, I'll be inside cleaning … If you need me." She turned to walk away, and then turned back. She had made progress after all, and she needed to acknowledge him for that. "Oh, and Elijah? Thank you for loading up your truck with the bags. I really appreciate it."

Elijah pinched the edge of his tan Stetson, the cowboy version of 'You're welcome,' and went back to collecting his eggs.

Chapter Six

Bea had opened both doors and every window she could find on the first floor to let the air filter through, with or without Elijah's permission. She was about an hour into reorganizing the kitchen cabinets that she'd previously left in neat piles, when she heard a car door outside, and the unmistakable click of heels on the front porch. Bea's heart sank as she peeked around the edge of the door to see who the intruder was.

The most beautiful woman she'd ever seen was stepping across the threshold, like she'd clearly been here plenty of times before. "Elijah?" the woman called out, looking for Bea's future husband.

She was tall, a good foot over Bea and a few inches shorter than Elijah, with flowing auburn-red hair, like the sunset in the fall. With high cheekbones and a well-tailored gray pantsuit, she looked like she could be a movie star, and Bea guessed that would be fitting, since Hollywood filmed here often.

The screen door opened behind Bea, and Elijah and Evelyn stepped inside. He noticed Bea first, whose head was still hung around the edge of the kitchen door. A play of amusement sparkled in Elijah's eyes as he followed her line of vision towards Bea's competition.

"Elijah! There you are!" The woman started walking down the hall towards him.

"Sorry, been here long? Lost track of time." He moved past Bea, who stood up straight and stared at the floor. She suddenly felt more like an intrusive child than a twenty-two-year-old woman trying to win the heart of the man she loved. And she was definitely going to rethink her wardrobe choices from now on.

The woman walked into the kitchen, noticing Bea instantly. "Oh! Is that your car in the driveway? It's adorable!" the woman complimented her. She was instantly warm and friendly, and Bea reminded herself that this could possibly be the enemy.

"Millie's granddaughter," Elijah offered, with no further explanation.

Well, that didn't make sense. If this woman and her grandma knew each other and knew that she was with Elijah, Millie certainly wouldn't have let Bea go and make a fool out of herself for nothing.

Bea held out her hand to shake the enemy's. "I'm on my way to her place next, as a matter of fact. Goodness, where are my manners? I forgot to introduce myself, and we both know Elijah here won't do me any favors, that's for sure." She winked at Bea, and Elijah huffed as he stood over the open refrigerator. "I'm Simone Lafitte. Pleasure to meet you!" She tilted her head slightly, signaling Bea to continue their exchange.

"Bea St. Claire. I'm here for the summer before I graduate." Elijah passed by the both of them, carrying several milk crates.

"What's your major?" Simone asked.

"Art. I'm an artist. I'm up here to sketch Elijah and the landscape, but I got sidetracked."

"Oh! Do you do murals, Bea? I'm going to need a muralist in the not-too-distant future."

"How many?" Elijah interrupted, now standing at the refrigerator with his milk crates.

"Whatever you've got is fine. Don't be rude. I'm in the process of hiring your … friend, here." She smiled at Bea knowingly, and Bea felt a wash of relief. Simone was not her enemy after all. That title was still one-hundred percent Elijah's.

"I haven't yet, but I could," Bea replied, more cheerily now that she was on level ground.

"Excellent! Tell you what, Bea. Email me your portfolio whenever you have time." She handed Bea her business card. "And when you're ready to look for jobs, we'll set something up! I'm so excited!"

She hugged Bea while Elijah stood there, holding three milk crates full of eggs in his long arms. Simone glanced at Elijah, not missing a beat. "Be a doll and load those into my trunk, would you?" She pulled her keys out of her purse and clicked a button. A *beep beep* sounded in the front yard, and Elijah groaned as he walked past them.

"This is good. This is great, I'm so happy you're here," Simone squealed in delight. She looked around the kitchen. "This is fabulous! You keep him on his toes, OK? Evelyn!" She looked around for the dog while she dug through her purse.

Evelyn immediately responded to her name, and came back in the kitchen to sit in front of Simone like they'd done this a million times. "You know I can't forget my girl!" She pulled out a plastic baggie of brightly colored dog treats, like those fancy gourmet bakery ones. Evelyn licked her lips as her chocolate dog eyes widened in delight.

"Evelyn, sweetie, you've got a feather stuck in your ear hair. Were you chasing Thelma again?" Evelyn's eyes shifted to the floor in guilt. "Well, I'm sure she deserved it." Simone handed Evelyn a pink iced dog bone dipped in sprinkles. She leaned over to Bea and put her hand to her mouth, whispering, "Thelma's the bitchy one. But Elijah loves them all equally."

Elijah came back into the kitchen. "Anything else?"

Simone pulled a brownie out of her purse. "I don't think so, but Mom sent this for you. It's turtle. Brownie of the Month."

She turned back to Bea. "If you need a summer job, let me know, all right?"

"She's at Rhonda's," Elijah offered.

Simone rolled her eyes. "OK, so *when* you need a summer job, let me know. I own The Avocado Taco, and I manage the in-house restaurant at the Tutwiler Springs Hotel. Whatever shift you'd like, we could work you in somewhere." Bea smiled and nodded.

After Simone had gone, Elijah cut the brownie and offered half to Bea. Bea's heart swelled as she graciously took it from him, wanting to savor every second of this experience. It tasted like heaven, and not because it was delicious, which it was, but because it was given to her by an actual angel.

"Who was she, again?"

"Simone. Owns a restaurant." The brownie turned hard in her throat. Bea decided she was going to do a series of rapid-fire questions if all she was going to get was minimal answers.

"Why was she here?"

"Eggs. The Avocado sources local."

"Do you think she's pretty?"

Elijah shrugged. "Never noticed."

Bea's eyes widened. "You've never noticed that she practically looks like a supermodel? That there was a supermodel standing in your kitchen?"

"Not my type, I guess. Known her all my life. Ben was sweet on her back in grade school." Bea did a double take. He'd just spoken a full sentence to her.

"As you may have heard, I'm not actually here to clean your house, Elijah. That's just a bonus for you. I came up here to ask if I could sketch you."

"Said as much." *Aaand we're back.*

"So, you'll let me sketch you? And your land?"

"Don't see why not."

Bea felt like they were actually having a conversation. All of his guards seemed to be somewhat down, even if he was mostly only giving her a few words at a time. "You cleaned for me. I can help you."

Bea almost peed herself from the excitement coursing through her body. "Can you give me a tour of everything? So I can map out locations? I'd like to start at the mine."

"No," he said coarsely. A shadow crossed his handsome face as he stared at her, his eyes ablaze with something unreadable.

She took a step back. Bea had crossed some line, but she didn't know what or how. "N-no what?"

"Don't ever go to the mine," he growled at her. Sensing the tension that had suddenly fallen in the room, Evelyn went to sit by Elijah. "It's closed."

"Yep, great. No mine, got it." Bea swallowed hard, the brownie still partly lodged in the base of her throat. "Could I have some milk, please?"

Elijah opened the refrigerator and got out an old-fashioned-looking glass jar full of milk. "You make your own milk, too?" Bea asked, watching him open each door of the newly reorganized cabinets until he found the glasses.

"No. Cows do, though." He snickered, his back still turned to her. Bea realized he was making fun of her, and she liked it. She liked that he was interacting with her at all.

"Oh, I see. Tough cowboy's got jokes for days." He handed her the glass, and their fingers lightly touched. She took a swig of the cold milk. It rushed down her esophagus, cooling her insides immediately and putting out the flame he'd ignited in her, yet again. She stared at the milk, trying not to focus on the fact that he was still standing in front of her. A few seconds of awkward silence passed between them.

"You get choked?"

That almost made Bea choke in itself. "No, I'm fine. Did you pasteurize this yourself?" She really knew nothing of how all of this worked, or what cowboys did other than ride off into the sunset.

"Whole Foods." Elijah was as close to a full grin as she'd seen him so far.

Bea squeezed her eyes shut, trying to make herself disappear. "Right. I have another question."

"Make it count. Gotta get to work." She wasn't sure if he was talking about her or him getting to work.

"I heard you outside, with the chickens. You were having practically a whole conversation …" she paused for dramatic effect, "with a *chicken*. How come?"

He smirked at her, amused, and stroked his long scraggly beard. "How come what?"

"How come you can have a whole conversation with a chicken, but not with me?" Bea's tone was halfway pleading, halfway whining. She'd never admit to anyone how jealous she was of a foul.

"Chickens are easier."

Bea nervously concentrated on sipping her milk, pretending to be completely fascinated by it, while Elijah stared at her. Finally, when Bea looked up to make eye contact with him, he clicked his tongue at Evelyn and turned to leave.

Bea stood there, unsure of how to feel, listening to their footsteps grow softer until she heard the roar of Elijah's truck start up and drive off.

Chapter Seven

They had developed a silent system—Bea would pile trash bags up on the porch, and Elijah would haul them away to the landfill. Three weeks later, with five weeks to go—not that Bea was counting down or anything—she had cleaned up nearly all that she was going to clean up. For free, anyway. If he wanted more, he'd have to pay her. And since he'd firmly said that wasn't happening, she was going to dedicate the last five weeks to building her portfolio.

Yesterday, after a long day of ranching, Elijah had returned, only to be confronted by an irritated Bea, who was having trouble understanding where her love story had gone wrong. Rhonda's words echoed in her brain every time she had any sort of negative thought about the situation she had found herself in.

S.T.O.M.A.C.H.

"How old are you?" It was about 4 p.m. on a Thursday when Bea accosted Elijah as soon as he entered the house. She was waiting for him, arms crossed and sitting on the old—but now clean—stairwell. He tromped into the hallway, closing the front door behind him, and kicked off his boots.

"Twenty-seven."

"All right." Her mouth fell open slightly, unsure of what to say next. The make-believe argument had sounded better in her head. He looked at her, expecting her to move out of his way. Bea stood up to let him by, but then shot her arm out to grip the banister, preventing Elijah from moving past. He was standing a full two stairs down from her, and they were now at eye level.

The smell of pure raw man and sweat enveloped her senses, and Bea had to force herself to concentrate. This close to him, she could see the fine lines starting to form around his eyes. And, from what she could tell, he barely had any laugh lines. *I guess that's the benefit of hardly talking. Or smiling.*

"No, actually, it's not all right." His hazel eyes met her Carolina blue ones. Bea felt a shudder down her back, and resisted the urge to reach out and wrap her arms around his neck and pull him into her. "I'm twenty-two. There's not that much difference between us, and you shouldn't treat me like such."

One of Elijah's eyebrows quirked up in a question. "Excuse me?"

"You heard me. We're the same, Elijah Callahan. Whether you like it or not. I'm done being your maid, do you hear me?" Bea's voice was getting squeaky. She stomped her foot on the stair. "I had this weird, twisted idea that by cleaning your house, I would earn my right to draw you, and I'm telling you, I'm done now. I'm going to spend the rest of my time working on my portfolio. You owe me some drawings."

Elijah crossed his arms and leaned his hip against the banister, the fascination still playing across his face. "Didn't ask you to be my maid."

"No, you didn't. And I'm not going to be anymore. I'm done with that and I'm moving on. You should notice me for my value as a person, not as a cleaning service."

Elijah took his hat off, and dropped it over the rail to the table just below. "You done?" He ran a hand through his long, dark blond hair. He didn't even have hat hair, which made Bea a whole new level of furious-for-no-reason.

"Yes, I'm done. I just wanted us to be on the same

page." Bea hmphed.

Elijah, clearly entertained at her tantrum, grinned and moved closer to her just to watch her squirm. "You coming back tomorrow?"

"I don't know." Bea's eyes shifted to the wall beside her to distract herself from how close he had leaned in.

"Come back at four. Wear something more practical than that." Elijah moved past her, their arms brushing against each other. Bea looked down at her cartoon T-shirt, ripped shorts, and flip-flops. She didn't know whether to be excited that she maybe had a date, or infuriated that he didn't like her clothing choices.

Chapter Eight

Later that night, the second Thursday of the month, punctual Ben Camden pulled up to the Callahan ranch at 5:30 on the dot. He was wearing his favorite blue Hawaiian shirt, along with cargo shorts and flip-flops.

Ben and Elijah had been best friends since they were little, from daycare onwards. Ben was the only one in town who could fully read Elijah like a book, and knew pretty much everything there was to know about him. Even when life got in the way, which it did more frequently since Ben had been promoted to lead detective at the police department last year, he and Elijah still maintained their second Tuesday boys' night. Which usually consisted of beer and s'mores.

Ben got out of his unmarked car, and Evelyn raced to greet him. He was her second-favorite person in the world, and he didn't even have to bribe her with fancy dog biscuits. She had been a gift from Ben to Elijah when she was just a puppy, after his grandpa had died. Evelyn was named after Ben's grandma, who had constantly watched over and/or babysat the duo when they were toddlers into their early teens.

"Holy moly, girl, what happened? You should've called me! I would've brought the whole force out here!" Evelyn jumped and barked, and Ben imagined she was laughing at his hysterical sense of humor. Elijah opened the door and walked out onto the porch. Freshly showered, he was now sporting a white undershirt and jeans, with his long hair loosely pulled back into a ponytail.

"Someone hauled away all your junk!" Ben looked around, grinning in amazement at the front yard, which was now sporting only a few old cars and car parts. He popped the trunk to get the groceries he'd brought.

Detective Camden rarely asked a question he didn't already know the answer to. Privy of this information, Elijah just held the door open and patted Ben on the back as he entered. Evelyn happily trotted in behind him.

"Dude." Ben walked into the kitchen, admiring it like he'd just walked into the biggest gun store known to man.

"Yeah," was all Elijah offered.

"The last time I was here, it was …" Ben was at a loss for words.

"Yeah."

"That was four weeks ago, and in that time all this happened?" He proceeded to rub oil on the potatoes, sprinkle Italian seasoning on them, cut them in halves, and wrap them in foil.

"Yep."

Ben squeezed Elijah's shoulder while he pounded their steaks with a meat cleaver. "I'm really proud of you, bro."

"Yep."

Elijah dumped the steaks into a bowl and poured marinade over them. Then, he grabbed the six pack, while Ben grabbed the potatoes and the bags of toppings and s'mores ingredients. They headed out to the pavilion.

In the furthest reach of the backyard, past the maple grove and the chicken coop, Elijah had fashioned a mini pavilion beside his grandpa's old pond. A river stone floor, covered by a tin roof with varnished cedar tree trunk columns, created Elijah's mini oasis. And underneath was a handmade cedar bench, a handmade cedar table, two chairs handmade from branches, and the manliest grill and smoker that Elijah could find.

He and Ben had built it a year after his grandpa died, when Elijah had needed something to root him back to the earth and keep him from spiraling. A lighted ceiling fan hung in the middle, to create a breeze on the hotter days. The only other lighting source out here was the sunset, and a large firepit he and Ben had constructed beside the pond.

Bea hadn't yet seen this side of him, or of his house. Nobody had seen this place except Ben. This was the only area on the whole entire property that was one-hundred percent unfiltered, unprotected Elijah Callahan. Simplistic and natural.

plop

plop

plop

Mom!!!!!!!! *Mooommmmm!!!!!!!* *Mmmooooommmm!!!!!*

A series of sequential splashes and screams from

the bullfrogs sounded into the pond when Ben poured lighter fluid into the end of the firepit and dropped the match. The bullfrogs weren't keen on having company, and completely hated anything at all being close to them. Ben and Elijah had long since decided that they were screaming "Mom!" and tattling because someone had disturbed their peaceful froggy existence.

The fire roared to life on one side of the pit. They kept it smaller in the summer, for s'mores and lighting purposes only, rather than the added benefit of warmth.

Ben went and got one of the branch chairs, and positioned it beside the fire. Elijah fired up the propane grill, added the potatoes, closed the lid, and set the timer.

"I'll wait about twenty, then add the meat." He pulled the other chair out beside Ben's.

The men sat there silently, as men so often do. They sipped their beers and listened to the bullfrogs complain. When Elijah got up to add the steaks to the grill, Ben got up and followed him.

"So, somebody broke in and started cleaning?" Ben asked smugly, while he took his place on one of the cedar benches.

"Something like that." Elijah didn't meet his gaze. He had known his friend long enough to know that he was monitoring his every move.

"Who is she?"

"Millie's granddaughter." Elijah kept his back turned, focusing hard on the grill.

"You hired her to clean your house?"

"No."

"She just came out here and started cleaning?"

"Yep."

"How long have you been seeing her?" Ben knew the only way to get a rise out of Elijah was to throw him a curve ball.

"What? I'm not. We're not together."

Ben took a long swig of his beer, and then popped open another one. "Women are a mystery. But if I've learned one thing from being married, it's that women don't clean an entire house or property unless they're pissed off at the world, pissed off at someone, or workin' through something deeply personal. Which is it?"

"Wouldn't know. Never asked."

"She cute?"

"Didn't notice. You want medium?" Elijah flipped the steaks, still careful to not make eye contact.

"Sure. What color's her hair?"

"Blonde."

"About how tall is she? I saw a blonde girl the other day I didn't recognize."

"Probably 5'5. She's working over at Rhonda's, too."

"What's she in town for?" Ben reached his arms behind his back and leaned against the table. Elijah was already sunk, and he didn't even know it yet.

"Summer break till she goes back to AU."

"Oh yeah? What's her major?"

"Art. She's an artist. Might get a job with Simone later."

"You noticed all that, but you didn't happen to notice if she's cute or not?"

Elijah glanced over his shoulder at Ben. "That's entrapment."

"Nah, that's just common sense. You were bound to find yourself a woman one of these days. It's been a while since Jen."

Jen had been Elijah's high school girlfriend, who, come to fine out, had only been with him for what she thought he could do for her. Once his life had completely shattered, she was right out the door with the rest of his hopes and aspirations. He ignored Ben's comment and threw it back to him with an equally sore subject.

"How's Tiffany?" Elijah plated the steaks and potatoes.

"Still Tiffany. Still teaching yoga. She's taking on more classes, I'm taking on more shifts. My advice, find somebody with the same goals in life who you can stand to be in the same room with for more than an hour. It'll work out better for you."

"Have you filed for divorce yet?"

"No. I don't want to be that guy, you know? The loser who gets divorced from his college sweetheart. Like who does that? Doesn't that defeat the purpose? Anyway, I think we're about to start going to counselling. She hasn't said it yet, but I think that's where we're heading." Ben made a fake gagging sound, scoffing at the idea of asking for help from a counsellor, while he opened up the potato condiments. "I remembered the bacon bits this time."

"Maybe we should grill bacon next time."

Ben froze midair, with the sour cream lid in one hand and the container in the other. "Is that a thing that people do?"

Elijah shrugged. "Could be. Never hurts to try."

"My man. I like this new and improved Optimistic Elijah."

Elijah just shook his head, hiding his grin.

"You don't have to hide from me. She's already changed you." Ben paused to look at him, before removing the foil from his potato.

"She hasn't. There's nothing to change and we're not together."

"When are you seeing her again?" A handful of cheese fluttered onto the table, missing Ben's plate altogether.

"Hope you shoot better than you dress your food. People's lives depend on it." Elijah passive-aggressively sprinkled cheese onto his potato, every shred landing perfectly inside the steam.

"Ha. I noticed how you just evasively answered a direct question."

Chapter Nine

"I'm gonna start a barbeque restaurant called Swine in a Comforter. It'll have fancy stuff, like devilled eggs, twice-baked potatoes, and ambrosia salad. And the tagline will be 'Pigs in a Blanket's ritzy rich city cousin!' Or something like that. What do you think?" Rhonda asked. She threw back a handful of popcorn, crunching it loudly while she continued to talk.

"It should probably have Swine in a Comforter on the menu, too. Like a featured appetizer. Maybe all-beef hotdogs wrapped in croissants. That sounds fun, right? And maybe some snazzy honey mustard smeared on there, too. I should call Simone about this, maybe we could partner up. There should be a job where I get paid to think up restaurant concepts."

She kept rambling before Bea could answer. Not that Bea had many opinions as of current. She was too focused on the ball of nerves accumulating inside her stomach. To distract herself, Bea had taken to breaking up the frozen ice in the back of the ice machine for the last thirty minutes while Rhonda spouted every thought in her head.

"I said, what do you think?" Rhonda crunched down on another handful. Bea's knees ached from crouching down for so long. She slowly stood up from the ice machine, metal scoop in hand.

"Sounds great, Rhonda. It would probably bring in a lot of people."

Rhonda's eyebrows matted. "Why're you so quiet today? What's the latest scoop from Lover's Lane?"

Bea thought better than to involve Rhonda, but then she decided against it. "I may or may not have a date tonight."

"Dear Lord in Heaven! I think a popcorn kernel's done attached itself to my uvula like a condom." Rhonda started coughing and hacking dramatically. "You got that man to ask you out? Tell me all the details!"

Bea ran her hand nervously through her ponytail, twirling it around her fingers as she sighed. "Maybe he asked me out? He said to wear something more practical than my usual shorts and T-shirt. Really, that was about all that was said. He was so close to me, though; if he said anymore I didn't hear it for the blood pounding through my ears."

"Exactly how close was he?" Rhonda leaned on the counter, raising her eyebrows. She tipped her nose down so far her glasses nearly slid off.

"Close. Close enough for me to question if I'd forgotten deodorant or not."

"Did he kiss you, honey? Or say anything else?"

Bea sighed. "No, he hasn't kissed me. Other than in my fantasies. I don't know, Rhonda. Sometimes I think he's clueless, and sometimes I think he's just playing with my emotions."

"That's the gift all men have, honey. You can't tell if they're purposely stupid or stupidly purposeful. When is this big maybe happenin'?"

"This evening. He wanted me to wear something more practical. What do you think that means?"

"Oh, honey!" She clapped her hands together and jumped up and down. "*That* means you need to go *shoppin'*! What're you still doin' here?"

Bea stared at Rhonda, wide-eyed, as if Rhonda didn't understand that she was Bea's boss.

"Girl, don't look at me like that." Rhonda waved her hand dismissively. "Lunch rush is over anyway, and you've got to *go*! Get on over to Cavender's and pick you out something snazzy and Western that'll make that boy's weird little heart stop in his chest. Go on!"

She wheeled Bea around by her shoulders and snatched the bow of her apron, whipping it off dramatically before shoving Bea towards the exit.

At the store, Bea decided by 'practical,' Elijah probably didn't mean the cute red and purple paisley sundress with capped sleeves that she was currently eyeing. She hung it on her arm anyway, and continued shopping until she found the perfect pair of jeans that would look great with her brown ankle boots.

Bea also found a blue plaid blouse that buttoned up to a frilly little V-neck collar that was the definition of cowgirl chic, if she had ever heard such a thing. Come to think of it, she actually hadn't heard such a thing, but that was the newly created style she was now aiming for. Cowgirl chic. *Otherwise known as chicken whisperer chic*, Bea thought to herself.

She tried everything on to make sure they fit
perfectly in all the right places, and then rushed back
to her grandma's house to change. Bea was nearly
out of time before she needed to head up to Elijah's,
so she applied some powder foundation and a nude
lip-gloss. She did a quick spin in the mirror,
appreciating how her new jeans hugged her hips and
angled into her waist just right. Then, Bea grabbed
her backpack and headed off to her maybe-first-date
with the man of her dreams.

~

The front door was open when Bea pulled up,
expecting of her arrival. When the car motor
stopped, Evelyn's furry paws jumped up to push the
screen door open. By the time it had slammed closed
with a *thwack*, Evelyn had already barreled into Bea
at full speed, nearly knocking her over.

"Hey, girl! It's only been a day, but I'm glad you
missed me, too." Bea glanced around. Elijah's truck
was parked outside, but he was nowhere to be seen.
She knew he was close, though, because Evelyn
wouldn't let him too far out of her sight.

Bea's boots made a thumping sound as she walked
up the stairs, practicing swaying her hips seductively
with each step. She shook her head, fluffing her hair

out so that the tresses fell loosely down her shoulders before she opened the screen door. Evelyn rushed in first, and back towards the kitchen.

Even though there were several hours of daylight left outside, the house was dark except for the light streaming down the hallway from the kitchen.

Bea headed that way, hearing the clink of silverware being dropped into the sink. When she walked around the corner, she gasped. She didn't think she would ever get used to seeing the beauty that was Elijah Callahan, but today was something different.

Today, unplanned as it was, they were wearing nearly matching shirts. His didn't have a frilly neck, of course, but the blue plaid was nearly the same. Bea took that as an encouraging sign from the universe. *Kismet.*

Elijah was standing over the sink, hair pulled back into a loose ponytail, with his trademark hat, boots, and jeans that made Bea's mouth water.

And he was … *making sandwiches?*

He delicately wrapped them in paper towels, inserted them into plastic bags, and then placed the carefully wrapped sandwiches into a large cooler.

Was this dinner? Elijah Callahan was *fixing dinner for her?*

Bea tried not to get excited. The Negative Nancy on her shoulder said, *It's just a ham sandwich, you idiot,* while the Positive Polly said, *You go, girl! Get that lunch meat!*

Evelyn looked back at Bea, and Elijah followed her gaze. His eyebrows raised as his eyes traveled slowly, from Bea's ankle boots all the way up her body until he reached her hair. Bea twirled around so he could fully see her, taking care to pop her hip out just a tad in case he hadn't noticed how her new jeans hung on her hips like they'd been shrink wrapped.

"Is this practical enough?" Bea asked cheerfully, and her heart lurched in her chest when she saw him gulp. *Yes, girl, you did it!* Positive Polly cheered.

Elijah looked back down at the cooler and rearranged the items in it. "Bring your pastels?"

"How do you know about pastels?" Bea asked, nearly in a whisper. She was shocked that he was speaking her language.

"Googled it," Elijah muttered, not bothering to look up at her again. "Can you walk in those?" He glanced back down at her feet, frowning.

Bea didn't know whether to be touched that he'd googled her interests, or furious that he still thought she was impractical. "Yes, I can, as a matter of fact. Technically, they're not higher than kitten heels. Which are *highly* practical." She stomped her foot, just for good measure.

Elijah snickered, and grabbed the cooler. He walked up to Bea, so close that the very tips of his long, scraggly beard brushed against her nose as he looked down at her. "All right, then. Let's go."

The scent of pine and maple and cedar and all things man and wonderful filled Bea's senses. If she knew anything about Elijah Callahan, it was what he smelled like on a normal basis vs. what he smelled like right now. Which was his normal scent, combined with the soap version of love at first sight. Elijah had showered for her, another step in the right direction.

Her eyes glazed over at his proximity, as her heart reached out through her chest to touch his. Bea focused on his full, lush lips buried beneath the scruff. If he didn't kiss her soon, she was going to explode.

She moved out of his way, careful to not let him see her gripping the door frame for support until she found her footing. If he was going to be up in her personal space, maybe kitten-heeled ankle boots weren't a practical choice after all.

Bea heard his uneven footsteps tread down the back stairs, and then a muffled, "You coming?"

She said a silent prayer for herself. *God, please grant me the strength to not spontaneously combust in front of this man. I'd really appreciate it.*

Then, Bea let go of the wall and headed out the back door to follow the man of her dreams into the great unknown.

Chapter Ten

… and about an hour later, she was still following him. Bea's feet were seriously starting to hurt, and even though Elijah hobbled, he obviously didn't let that hold him back at all. He had been outpacing her by about five steps the entire time.

Bea huffed and puffed as they continued up the mountain. "Can you please slow down? Can we like, stop, or something? I can't breathe!"

Elijah slowed, but only slightly. "Running low on daylight."

"Yeah, OK, I get that. But I'm running out of lung power. Seriously low." Bea shut her eyes and wheezed hard, and crashed into Elijah's back.

"You got a camera on your phone?" Elijah turned around and handed Bea a bottle of water he'd retrieved from the cooler. She doubled over, wrapping her palms around the back of her knees to try and catch her breath.

Bea's bangs were completely plastered to her forehead, and she knew, *just knew*, that her previously fluffed and sexy hair was now wet strings around her face. She pulled a hairband from her backpack and quickly threw her hair up into a bun, secretly praying that it landed on the sexy side of hot mess. She glanced up at Elijah, her eyes narrowing in the furious realization that his skin was barely glistening, while she was sporting the full-on wet mop setting.

"On my phone," she huffed again, her steady breath starting to come back to her now.

"You'll probably have to take pictures when we get there. I thought you'd be able to make it up the hill." He turned and started walking again, without asking if she was ready.

Rage flew all over Bea at his snarky remark. "Hey!" Elijah kept walking, and she couldn't be sure, but she thought maybe he'd quickened his pace just to piss her off.

"HEY!" Bea screamed. Elijah slowed.

"First of all, I am in *fabulous* shape. Second of all, this is not a hill. It's a mountain. An actual, snow-in-the-distance-for-whatever-reason-even-though-this-is-Texas mountain."

Elijah just looked at her while she had her breakdown, with a sly, barely noticeable grin beneath his beard. "If you need me to carry you, just ask."

Bea's mouth fell into an O shape while she mentally pooled into a mortified puddle.

"Aaahhhhh!" she screamed in his general direction, because her brain was too exhausted for snappy comebacks. Bea stomped past him and onwards up the mountain, ignoring his shaking shoulders while he openly laughed at her.

~

Elijah had quickly caught up and surpassed Bea again, and by the time he finally stopped, her pink, pained toes were throbbing inside her boots.

"We're here," was all he said as he headed over to a flat rock and sat the cooler down. They had ended up on a flat, grassy clearing on top of the mountain. Bea took the opportunity to strip her boots off and stretch her toes out. She headed over to Elijah and sat down on the rock, with the cooler between them.

"You all right?" he asked, faking genuine concern, though Bea knew deep down he was probably mocking her.

"I don't want to talk about it. Where are we?" She massaged her toes while she surveyed their surroundings for the first time. "And how will we get back?" Thankfully, the path they had taken had been relatively flat, so the risk of Bea actually snapping her neck while she tumbled back down the mountain was relatively low. Still, with her luck, she didn't want to gamble more than she needed to.

"I brought flashlights." Elijah opened the cooler and started laying the items out behind them on the rock. Bea was too busy looking around to notice all he'd brought for them.

The sun was starting to set, and the pinks and magentas of the sky were swirling together with the blues overhead. It was the most beautiful, and romantic, thing Bea had ever seen, and the fact that Elijah had been the one to bring her here warmed chambers of her heart that she hadn't known had existed.

From where they sat, she could see the unmistakable horseshoe shape of Goodwater Falls in the distance, and all the lights from the main part of town. She could even see the soft glow from the arena and stadium on the other side of town, closer to the smaller Knickabrick Falls, from which the local NHL team got their name. Elijah's farmhouse was just a little white dot below them, which spoke to the true size of the Falls. Bea had never actually seen the Falls up close, but maybe Elijah would take her there, as well.

"Ham or turkey?" Elijah asked, bringing her out of her daydreams.

"Ham, please." Bea carefully unwrapped the sandwich that Elijah handed her, trying to memorize every detail of every aspect of their date, sans throbbing toes.

Elijah handed her another bottle of water, and a sleeve of crackers.

"What're these for?" Bea asked, confused.

"I got hummus," was his reply. He popped the top off of the container, and handed it to her.

"You got hummus?" Bea asked, still confused. Elijah was *so not* a hummus type of man.

"Garlic. And chocolate. Seemed like something you'd like."

Bea's heart swelled large enough to fill her ribcage. Elijah had thought of her. He'd gone *shopping* for her.

She really was making progress. She re-prayed her previous prayer. *Dear God, please do not let me spontaneously combust and ruin this hummus.*

She wanted to cry, to hug him, to *kiss him* for being considerate and trying to impress her. Instead, she focused on the more obvious matter at hand. "I didn't know they made chocolate hummus."

"Guess they do." Elijah shrugged, and took a bite of his sandwich.

Bea mimicked him, biting into her ham for the first time. Her taste buds exploded into new flavors she wasn't expecting. "What'd you do? This is honestly the best ham and cheese I've ever had in my life!"

Elijah shrugged. "Just cream cheese. My grandpa called it his secret weapon. I got the herb one or whatever it was."

Well, well, well. Who knew Elijah Callahan had gourmet picnics up his sleeves? Bea didn't miss the fact that he'd mentioned his grandpa. "I'd say he was pretty clever. What happened to him, if you don't mind me asking?"

A shadow fell across Elijah's face, and Bea instantly regretted mentioning anything about his past. Come to think of it, she really didn't know anything about him at all, and she had no clue what topics were and were not off limits for him. She dropped the subject immediately, and stared at the fine line of speckled herb cream cheese oozing out from between the bread and the cheddar cheese of her sandwich.

They ate in silence for a few minutes. Evelyn sat at her feet, patiently waiting for a strip of crust. "You better start taking pictures," Elijah finally muttered beside her.

Bea took out her phone and her sketchbook. "Undo your hair. Fluff it around some, like how it'd be on a normal day. And look off in the distance, like you're thinking really hard." He obeyed her, and Bea started snapping photos of him, of the sunset, of his perfect profile. She zoomed the lens of her phone slightly, accentuating the outline of his biceps beneath the blue plaid. Her throat went dry, and she took a long swig of water.

"I am," Elijah stated after a minute of Bea clicking away.

"What? You are what?" She drew out a rough sketch to lay her groundwork. Bea admired his features, his adorable profile and gently sloping nose that ended in a subtle roundness. Bea wished she could see his lips. She imagined their shape, two perfectly luscious cupid's bows just waiting to introduce themselves to her ever-patient ones. Evelyn hopped up on the opposite side of him, her dog snout moving forward and trying to frame his face.

"Thinking hard." He glanced over at her.

"Keep your head facing forward. You can talk, but face the same direction." Bea circled her finger around, invisibly steering him back.

"You always so pushy?"

"Yes. But only when I see something I want." Bea heard a voice talking, that sounded like hers, but the inner Bea would never have been so bold. This imposter Bea was full on, blatantly flirting.

"You don't want me," Elijah said flatly, as a statement of fact.

"You don't get to tell me what I want, last I checked." If Bea knew one thing in her twenty-two-year life span, it was that she absolutely *did* want this man.

"You're not scared?"

"You asked me that before. What am I supposed to be scared of?"

"Me." His eyes shifted back to her. Bea responded by swirling her finger back at him again.

"What about you? Your hobbling? That's hardly somethin' to get up in a fuss about."

"That the rumors are true."

"I don't think they are. I'm an excellent judge of character and you are a sweet, kind man, Elijah. Frustrating, yes, but not dangerous."

Bea continued to sketch, and Elijah continued to stay silent, until the sun had nearly set.

When Elijah had decided they'd had enough, he fished the flashlights out of the cooler. "Wrap it up."

Bea's heart broke, devastated that their evening on top of the world was over. She felt like so much, and yet, so little, had happened in their short evening. She was glad it was dark, so he couldn't see the disappointment on her face.

He pointed around until the light found her boots in the dark. "You good?"

"Yep. Yep, no problems here." Bea was going to have the worst blisters of her life tomorrow, but she would never ask Elijah to carry her an hour and a half back down the mountain. She knew if she did, only one of two things could happen.

Possibly, her pride would die and she'd never be able to look at him. Or, worse still, no matter what position he carried her in, honeymoon or piggyback, she'd never be able to remove her arms from around him.

Either way, Bea would lose.

Chapter Eleven

"But he kissed you, right? Please tell me that boy finally kissed you." Rhonda smacked her gum loudly while she prepped the lemons. Her beehive hair was lilac purple this week.

"Well, no. We just sort of … waved and that was it. He opened my car door for me, though. That's something, right?"

"Dear sweet Lord in Heaven! Jerry, are you listenin' to this mess? No, absolutely no! That ain't nothin' if there's nothin' else to back it up. Sweet Jesus, you kids are givin' me a heart attack. It's a wonder the human race ever procreated at all, the way ya'll keep gabberin' on!"

Rhonda smacked Bea on her rear as she passed by her. "Honey, you're gonna have to put some sass in that ass in order to catch yourself a man. You can't keep bein' mousey about it." The kitchen door swung back and forth behind Rhonda as she disappeared out of sight.

Bea stood there, depressed and sad. They really had had a good night, even if it had only been as friends and nothing more. Even if the thought that it might never be more completely shattered Bea to her core.

The bell dinged that a new customer had entered, and Bea glanced up from her misery to put on a temporary smile. Only the man who had entered was staring directly back at her, before she could even catch her bearings.

He is extremely handsome, Bea thought. *Though obviously not as much as Elijah, but he still tips over to the freakishly attractive side of the scale. He's tall, taller than Elijah, with short, black hair. He has dusty blue eyes, and he's much skinnier and leaner than Elijah. Not that Elijah is fat or anything, he's just more filled out. Like a Ken doll.*

This man looked more like Jack Skellington in a suit. And not a well-fitted suit at that. It hung loosely on his thin frame, like he'd grabbed the first thing he could find in a department store and hadn't bothered to have it tailored.

He smiled at Bea, and she noticed he also had adorable dimples. The man sat down directly in front of her. He watched her like a hawk, and only broke his gaze when she offered him a menu. He wasn't creepy about it at all, but Bea felt … *How do I feel? Like I'm under interrogation?*

Rhonda burst through the door right as the man opened his menu. Bea noticed his shoulders sagged slightly as he sighed.

"Sakes afire! Benjamin! You're skinnier than a green bean and twice as long. Obviously you need to come here more often so I can take care of you properly. Do you want Jerry to add extra cheese to your burger?"

Before the man could answer, or even order something different, Rhonda screamed through the window, "Jerry, make it a double! Officer Camden here won't starve on my watch!"

She turned back around, squeezing her forearms inward to make her chest appear larger while she leaned over the counter to talk to him. "Now then, Officer Camden, to what do we owe this honor?"

"We've been over this, Rhonda. It's Detective Camden now. You know that."

"Maybe I just like hearing you say my name, *Detective*," Rhonda purred at him. "What else can I get you today? A slice of my Aphrodisiac Apple Pie?

How 'bout a piece of my Laced with a Love Spell Lasagna to go?"

"Keep on, and I'll take you in for assaulting an officer of the law," Ben said nonchalantly, as if this was a regular conversation between them.

"Benjamin, I didn't touch you. Unless you'd like me to, of course," Rhonda scoffed.

"No, I would not. You just asked if you could serve me laced food. In front of a witness, no less." He trained his eyes back on Bea, who had been thoroughly enjoying the show.

"Keyword being asked, as in, for your permission. I was not evasive about the process. I've been watchin' my true crime shows, Benjamin, and I'm privy to your ways now."

"Rhonda," Ben said exasperatedly.

"Oh hush, Benjamin. You're no fun." She grabbed Ben's plate from the window and set it down in front of him. She then squirted a ketchup heart onto a napkin and slid it towards him.

He ignored her love note. "Not aiming to be fun. Just came for lunch." Ben's eyes never left Bea's.

Rhonda sized Ben up, to see if she could push just a little further. "Jerry! Today might be the day!"

Bea broke her gaze from Ben to look at her manager. "The day for what?" he asked.

"The day I leave him for Ben here." Rhonda grinned, and Ben rolled his eyes.

"Today is not the day, Rhonda," Ben growled.

"Ah, but you admit the day will come! Oh, it's comin' all right! There's just somethin' about when you flash that badge at me that gets me all excited and then any eggs I have left start shootin' themselves out of my fallopian tubes like loaded nerf guns!"

"Rhonda!" Bea gasped. She was utterly humiliated, both for Detective Camden, who was slightly blushing from embarrassment, and from Rhonda's crass demeanor towards him.

"Detective, I am so sorry for her behavior. Truly, I am. We'll have a talk about it later, I can promise you that." Bea placed her hands on Rhonda's shoulders and steered her away from the counter. Ben was watching her take control of the situation with an amused expression on his face. Bea shoved

Rhonda through the kitchen door, out of his sight, and returned to apologize.

"No harm done, ma'am. Unfortunately, I'm used to it from her," Ben said. He finished his burger, while Bea kept her eye on the kitchen door to make sure Rhonda wouldn't come back out. The whole time, he watched Bea—her reactions, her interactions with other customers, the way she carried herself. When he got up to leave, he tipped her $20 and winked at her. Then he was gone.

Bea burst into the kitchen, where Rhonda was propped up against the wall and dropping ice cubes down her bra.

"Oh, Lordy, that man makes me feel like I'm goin' through menopause all over again."

Bea had nearly had enough. "Don't take this the wrong way, Rhonda, but you're old enough to be his grandma."

"Love knows no age, sugar." Rhonda fanned herself with her hands.

"Plus, you're married. Remember?"

"Honey, when you've been together as long as Jerry and I have, you start to understand each other in ways you never thought possible. Jerry would know how it was, the day Benjamin comes in here to whisk me away. We've discussed it. Same as I'll stand aside on the day Scarlett Johansson comes in here to sweep Jerry off his feet. We won't try to stop each other from livin' our dreams."

Bea stood there, in shock, not having any type of response.

Rhonda grinned at her. "Besides, sugar, we learned a lot today from Detective Camden's visit. He couldn't keep his eyes off of you, which means he was sizing you up."

"Sizing me up for what?"

"Honey, I know I told you but I'll tell you again. That man is your boyfriend's BFF. *Bee. Eff. Eff*," she enunciated slower a second time. "He may not be talkin' to you, but he's certainly talkin' to Benjamin. If you've made enough of an impression that Benjamin had to come down here and tolerate my advances just to see you for himself, that can only be a great thing as far as your love story goes."

~

The next day, Sunday, Bea was sitting beside her grandmother in church.

"Did you hear what Simone did?" Violet, her grandmother's best friend and the local librarian, whispered loudly enough for Bea to hear. The three of them were sitting on a pew, nearly towards the front, waiting for services to begin.

"Violet McGee, I've never known you to be a gossip," Millie said, jibing at her friend.

"Truth isn't gossip if her own mother told me. Pretty ballsy if you ask me. Call me crazy, but I think it's going to work out for them."

Bea's head was spinning, trying to put the name to a face. She needed to draw herself a tree map just to keep up with everyone in this town. *Who was Simone again?* Bea's eyes widened. Simone was the drop-dead gorgeous restauranteur who bought Elijah's eggs.

Bea leaned in closer, pushing her arm flush against her grandmother's to try and get more into the conversation. "What'd Simone do?"

Violet tilted her head down to peek above the top rim of her glasses as she flipped absent-mindedly through her hymnal. "It's a crazy love story. I wouldn't have believed it if Lillian hadn't told me herself. You know that movie that's shooting downtown? Well—"

A loud thwack landed beside Bea. Violet's gaze immediately went cold, glaring at the interruption.

"Bea! Bea! I've never with my own two eyes!" Bea's head whipped around at the commotion that could only be coming from Rhonda.

"Uuughhhh," Violet groaned, rather obviously, at Rhonda's presence. Millie angrily glared at Rhonda for disturbing the group's peace of mind.

"Hush it, you old biddie. I've got news here that Bea needs to know!"

Violet and Millie continued to shoot daggers while Rhonda scooted in further, squashing Bea to where she had to contort her shoulders forward and rest her forearms in her lap. "What is it, Rhonda?"

"Oh, honey, look in the back! Right beside my *handsome* Detective Camden," she said loud enough that anyone who was listening could hear. "It's none other than Elijah Callahan! In here! In church!"

Bea's heart galloped outside of her chest and ran back and forth between each pew while she tried to mentally remind herself that most everybody in this town goes to church. "And?"

"And? Honey, that boy doesn't come to church unless it's a holiday occasion. The last time he was here was at Easter service!"

Millie whispered beside Bea, attempting to be much more ladylike than Rhonda's boisterous nature. "She's right, Bea. Elijah doesn't usually make an appearance."

"Don't you see what this means, Bea? You're workin' him good, girl! Gettin' him out of his routine. It's got to be a fabulous sign." She slapped Bea's shoulder before getting up to rejoin Jerry several pews behind them.

Bea rubbed her shoulder, and turned her head to her grandma. She wanted desperately to look towards the back and find him, to see if it was true.

Darn Rhonda, now I won't ever be able to focus on the service no matter what Preacher Dan's talking about. He could practically have live baby lambs on stage and I would still be too preoccupied with where Elijah was, and if he was looking at me or if he'd seen me, and what this meant or if it meant anything, and if he was going to talk to me, or maybe if he'd just felt like going to church today.

"Gracious me, just turn around and wave at him.
The wheels in your head are giving me a migraine,"
Violet snapped, the chains on her glasses jiggling
along with her tone of voice.

"He's just a man, Bea," her grandmother said,
patting Bea's tightly clenched hands.

"No, he's not …" Bea's words were barely a
whisper. He was *her* man.

Bea worked up the courage to push the ball of
nerves in her stomach away and turn around. She
took a deep breath, before slowly pivoting in her
seat. *Why do church pews have to be so uncomfortable?* Her
knee hit the back with a loud thud, giving away her
gracefulness. Bea shook it off, and breathed in deep
again, trying to look as nonchalant as possible. Her
eyes surfed the crowd of people along the back pews
until they found Ben, a head and a half taller than
everyone else.

There, directly beside him, was her cowboy. Bea's
mouth fell open upon impact of her eyes hitting his.
His hazel and lightning eyes were staring back at her.
Unapologetically. Deliberately. Her gaze quickly
shifted to Ben, who winked at her and grinned,
before she whipped back around at lightning-fast
speed.

"Bea, you're going to have to work on your breathing or I'll have to get you an oxygen mask for Christmas. That's not healthy," Millie chided, and Violet snickered.

Bea nervously picked at her cuticles throughout the entire sermon. Ironically enough, the day's lesson was on 1 Corinthians. Bea couldn't decide if "Love is patient" was a sign, or His sense of humor. She, in fact, was running out of patience, and running out of summer.

Halfway through, two of her cuticles started bleeding, and Bea impatiently sucked at them to force a clot. Millie put her hand on Bea's forearm, calmly signaling for her to stop all of her twitching.

Bea wanted desperately to go sit with Elijah, to be near him, to see what he thought was his Sunday best, and to hear what his singing voice sounded like. *His singing voice?!*

There were so many layers to Elijah Callahan that Bea didn't know yet, and she was hanging on every detail she could, trying desperately to fill in the gaps in between with her own imagination.

On the flip side, she also semi-hated herself for being so strung up over a boy. This was not normal

Bea at all. Normal Bea had thrown mud balls out her second story window at any boy who dared to knock on her front door in grade school. Normal Bea had stayed home from both the junior and senior prom, because she'd rather curl up with Netflix and popcorn than put on make-up and a fancy dress. Normal Bea wasn't in a sorority, and had never been to a college party when the rest of her classmates were into the hook-up culture. Normal Bea hung out in the art studio until all hours of the night, creating beautiful things.

Though she had created many beautiful drawings, paintings, and sketches from her imagination, this was a different part of her altogether. Her heart had never actually felt anything like this. Anything like Bea in Love.

Bea in Love?

Yes. Bea in Love.

Now she had a title for her senior portfolio. Bea in Love. And she would most certainly *never* tell Elijah the name of it. That would *absolutely* be *too* forward. She'd save that story for their honeymoon. That would be a safe time to tell him.

She could keep going all day with the puns of her name. Why hadn't she thought of it before now? *Oh, Bea-have.* That was hilarious. She snickered in the middle of the closing prayer, and Millie swatted her knee.

As the crowd exited the church building, Bea kept her eyes glued to the back of Elijah's head. She was devastated to see him disappear through the white double doors, without giving her a second glance. The sunlight blinded her as she absently filtered out into the brightness.

There was no potluck today to keep the congregation around for longer than they needed to be. By the time Bea, Millie, and Violet had gotten out of the building, the cars in the dirt parking lot had already roared to life. Funnels of dust trailed out and melded into a steady stream aimed towards the highway.

Millie turned around to Bea, who was in turn trusting her grandmother to lead her to safety while her pupils returned to their normal size.

"I get the feeling that somebody would like to have a word with you, Bea-utiful." Millie grinned, that all-knowing grandmother grin, and nodded her head to the left. At the same time Bea's eyes found Elijah through the dirt clouds, a familiar, wet nose slid against the palm of her hand.

"Hey, girl, did you get lost?" She was grateful to the dog for providing her with an icebreaker to help overcome the blankness of thought whenever Elijah was in close proximity.

Evelyn wagged her tail, and turned to march back to her owner as if she were satisfied with the mission she'd set out to accomplish. Bea's heart palpitated out of her chest as the rest of the crowd cleared and she saw him fully for the first time.

Elijah's Sunday best was a clean version of his everyday attire—blue and yellow plaid long-sleeve button-up shirt and jeans, paired with his usual cowboy hat and boots. He was standing directly beside his truck, elbow relaxed on the front hood, legs crossed at the ankle, his bad foot relaxed flat against the tire.

Waiting for someone.

Waiting for Bea.

He watched her intently as she approached, the lightning blazing in his hazel eyes. Bea tucked her hands behind her back, conscious of her newly massacred cuticles, as she trotted up to him cheerily. Bea was glad she'd chosen to wear her light-green sundress, the one that swished when she walked and accented her in all the right places without being too revealing.

But Elijah noticed, nonetheless. Bea couldn't be sure, because of his beard, but she thought she saw his bottom lip tremble when she was just a few paces away.

Evelyn moved to sit beside him, patiently waiting for the two humans to interact. Her brown dog eyes moved back and forth, like, *Well? I did my part. Do I have to do everything?*

"You brought Evelyn to church?" Bea said, as steadily as she could without her voice cracking from nerves.

"Shepherd stories make her feel important," Elijah said, and Bea's nerves lightened immediately as she burst out laughing. Elijah grinned, and Bea looked down at the ground to keep from throwing herself into his arms.

"I guess they do. Shame she has to sit in the truck, though."

"She won't have it. She waits by the door, with her ear pressed against it to listen."

"Of course, nobody ever gets to pull a fast one over on Evelyn, right?"

"Reckon not."

They both stood there, the conversation hanging in the air between them as to what to say next. Evelyn thumped her tail loudly several times, causing puffs of dust to rise up. *Down here, dummies.*

Bea took her hint. "I haven't seen you here this summer."

"Don't come much, except on special occasions."

"Well, I'm glad Evelyn got you to come out. Dogs need Jesus, too. They say all dogs go to Heaven, you know."

"Makes sense."

Millie yelled from across the parking lot. "Bea! Hurry up! We want to get to the Taco before the lunch rush!"

Bea closed her eyes, silently cursing her grandma. Millie knew how important this moment was to Bea.

"All right, well, it was great to see you," Bea stuttered out. She gave him a limp, apologetic half smile and turned to leave.

"Wait," Elijah mumbled. Bea's heart soared to new heights. She turned back around to him. His head was tilted down, so she couldn't see his eyes for his hat.

"Yes?"

"I … We … Evelyn was wondering what your favorite movie was." Evelyn thumped her tail in agreement like she had, in fact, been wondering.

"*Gone with the Wind*," Bea said quickly. She didn't even have to think about it.

Elijah's head snapped up, his nose slightly wrinkled. "Isn't that like twelve hours long?"

"It is not. It's four," Bea defended.

"Same thing." Elijah shrugged, quickly relaxing back to his typical devil-may-care demeanor.

"No, it's not. And, it's the most romantic movie ever made. So, there's that. Plus, Clark Gable was wildly handsome, and Scarlett's dresses are iconic.

Did you ever see that episode of *The Carol Burnett Show*? Legendary."

"If you say so."

"I do. Listen, I've got to go or Violet and Millie are going to skin me alive. I'll see you around, OK?"

Elijah nodded, and Bea turned around to leave for the second time. She got about three steps away from him, before she heard his sweet, deep voice tangle into her senses again. "Friday?" he called.

Bea stopped, and turned around. "Friday?"

Elijah nodded. "Same time Friday? Four p.m.?"

Bea nodded and smiled politely, trying not to look too eager. "Same time Friday."

When she got to the car, Millie was watching her like a hawk. "Violet went ahead to get us a table. I'm guessing my little shenanigans had the desired effect, judging by the way you floated over here."

"You interrupted him on purpose?"

"Bea, sometimes men need to know that they're on a clock, and that you've got better things to do. At that moment, your options were simple. Either that man had to ask you out, or you were going to leave his company to eat chips and queso. No man likes to compete with chips and queso. And that is a fact. So, did he ask you out?"

"Maybe. He asked me to come back to his house Friday night. And he asked what my favorite movie was."

"Queso for the win."

Chapter Twelve

After the longest five days of Bea's life, Friday rolled around. She'd managed to keep herself preoccupied with her drawings, sketching the pictures of Elijah and the mountains she'd taken the previous Friday. She'd even painted several canvases. Bea was determined to keep herself busy and productive, and not sit by the window and pine away for her mysterious mountain man.

This second maybe-date felt somehow more monumental than the first. This one was most assuredly an actual date, or so Millie, Bea, and Violet had determined on Sunday over carnitas tacos.

The fact that he used Evelyn as a segue to conversation showed that he was nervous. The fact that he came to church showed he was willing to step out of his routine. And the fact that he had even bothered to speak to any woman at all showed how serious he must be about Bea. All that on top of the fact that Ben had come into the diner to scope her out and give her his silent approval. It had taken two bowls, not cups, of queso, and four baskets of tortilla chips to arrive at this conclusion.

On Thursday, at exactly 5:02 p.m., directly after the library closed, Violet had called Millie. After a hushed and short conversation, Millie hung up the phone and came upstairs to Bea's room.

"Make sure you wear something really nice. What was it he said? Practical? That man likes practical things, not hoity-toity. And wear your hair down."

On Friday, a mysterious phone call to the diner at lunchtime had prompted Rhonda, ever the sucker for a good romance story, to let Bea off two hours early so she could spend extra time getting ready.

With her surplus of time, Bea got ready for her second maybe-date. She took a shower and washed her hair. After it air-dried, she straightened it with her flatiron, making sure there were no flyaway kinks or any strands acting up. She ironed her bangs until they had just the right amount of swoop across her forehead. She applied a light mist of hairspray, to make sure there would be no unaccounted-for frizzing.

Bea applied light foundation, and nude lip gloss, much like she had the first time. She didn't like to overdo it too much, but she did decide to go with a slightly darkened eyeshadow just to make her eyes pop a little more. All week, Bea had been wearing her contacts, so tonight she opted for her glasses. The bit of eyeshadow complimented them well.

Next, she put on the same jeans she'd worn last week that had—or so she'd imagined—made Elijah have to catch his breath. She paired them with a Free People tunic top she'd found in a thrift store. It was her favorite, fanciest shirt, that she only brought out for special occasions. She put the ankle boots back on, but stuck her tennis shoes into her backpack just in case she needed them.

Before leaving, Bea did a quick spin in the mirror. Her style was practical hippie chic, and she was adorable. If her Free People tunic didn't make Elijah stop in his tracks, nothing would.

She didn't know what he had planned, so she grabbed her backpack of drawing supplies just in case, and headed out the door.

~

Bea walked up the porch stairs, to be met by none other than Evelyn, eternal door greeter. Bea headed down the dark hallway, towards the kitchen light and the heavenly smell of grilled meats.

When she turned the corner, she was greeted by silence, save for Evelyn's toenails clicking on the linoleum. The stove was turned on, set at a low temperature to keep something warm. Bea sat her backpack down by the table, then walked over to the oven. She leaned down and peered through the door, and came face to face with an aluminum pan, covered in more aluminum foil.

"The plot thickens," she whispered to Evelyn, while she scratched the dog behind her ears. "Where's your dad gone off to?"

The slamming of the screen door on the back porch answered her. In walked Elijah, and Bea's mouth watered even more. Just when she thought he couldn't be any more attractive to her, he always went and outdid himself without even trying. He was barefoot, with his long hair pulled back into a loose ponytail, sans hat, with low-slung carpenter jeans and a white V-neck undershirt that desperately tried to contain a wholesome image. If Bea's style was hippie chic, Elijah's had to be country hipster.

This version of Elijah was the most laid back one she had seen, and Bea secretly squealed with internal delight that he was feeling more comfortable with her.

"I'll ask again, do you want cheese or not?" Elijah asked, slightly raising his voice in case she was randomly hard of hearing.

"What? Oh, I'm sorry, I zoned out for a minute." Bea's cheeks flushed at her embarrassment. She'd been looking at how delicious the man was, that she hadn't even noticed he was holding a plate of aluminum foil-wrapped potatoes.

Elijah's hazel eyes twinkled with amusement. "So, cheese?"

"Yes, please."

She watched as he sauntered past her, placing the potatoes on the countertop. He gently unwrapped them with tongs, careful not to burn himself as the steaming hotness rolled out.

"Sorry I didn't meet you. Sometimes they take an extra minute," Elijah said, his back still to Bea while he sliced two potatoes in half and made a pocket in each. He moved to the refrigerator and took out butter, shredded cheese, and sour cream, and placed them on the counter.

Putting on an oven mitt, he turned to Bea. "You want bacon bits, too? They're grilled."

"Absolutely, I do. I'll take the works." Bea and Evelyn patiently watched Elijah dress each potato with topping before removing a slim, folded piece of aluminum foil. He was careful to hold it over the pan while he unwrapped it. Bea and Evelyn licked their lips while they watched the grease slowly drop back into the pan. Then, Elijah used the tongs to take out two pieces of what looked like grilled chicken and weeds out of the aluminum foil pan.

"I take it we're not hiking today?" Bea asked, her eyes glued to the chicken.

Elijah dropped his hand to his side, holding one piece of bacon down for Evelyn. She graciously chomped it in a single gulp.

"Thought you needed a break from last week." Elijah turned around, smirking, and faced Bea. He held a plate in each hand.

"I was fine. I made it," she muttered.

"Barely." Elijah grinned and nodded his head for her to follow him.

Bea had never been in the living room. It was big, dark, and dusty, and she realized that in all of her cleaning, she hadn't actually even touched this room. She'd been so preoccupied with the grounds, the kitchen, and the rooms Elijah seemed to use the most, that she had skipped this one completely. It wasn't really that cluttered, though. Not like the rest of the place had been.

Bea wouldn't have thought it was anything too terribly exciting, except that in front of the couch, two TV trays were opened and set up with paper towels and silverware. They weren't side by side, but they weren't on opposite ends of the couch, either.

There was a TV set, old enough to be boxy but not so old that it wasn't still a flat-screen as well. Bea quickly decided it was probably the first flat-screen ever made, bless his heart. Her heart warmed in his minimalist nature, before also noticing a small end table set up, with a DVD player hooked up to it. There was a sticker on the front that read "Property of Goodwater Ranch Library."

Bea's eyes widened at the realization that all of the secret phone conversations had amounted to this. Elijah Callahan didn't take stock in modern musings, so he would've had to rent a DVD player from the local library.

Which meant he got it from Violet McGee, her grandma's best friend. Which meant that after he'd left the library, Violet would have immediately called Millie. Then Millie, knowing Bea was at work, would have immediately called Rhonda and told her to let Bea off even earlier.

Crap.

So, basically the whole town knew about their date, and the lengths Elijah had gone to. Which was extremely adorable, and also an intense amount of pressure to be under if nothing happened. *Again.*

And now here she was, and here he was, with this extremely romantic meal that was way fancier than ham and cheese sandwiches with a hummus appetizer.

Bea sat down at one tray, Elijah at the other, and Evelyn in between them. Evelyn the Icebreaker.

"Coke, Mountain Dew, or bottled water?" Elijah asked.

"Mountain Dew. Always Mountain Dew." He reached down beside the couch and popped open what sounded like a giant cooler full of ice, and scrounged around until he pulled out two cans of soda, dripping with ice water.

Bea looked at her chicken, which had a twig of green sticking out of it.

"What is this?" she asked. She realized the answer to her question the same time as she asked it while removing the twig. The aromas of basil and rosemary enveloped her senses while she removed the greenery.

"Rosemary. Basil's in the middle, picked from the garden. My grandma used to do that every Friday night."

The thought of Elijah Callahan picking herbs from a herb garden was the only thing on this earth that was more adorable than a basket full of puppies and kittens. It was a nearly unbearable thought that made Bea's heart palpitate uncontrollably.

"Elijah … thank you so much. Your grandma must've been quite a woman. This is really fancy." Bea sliced into her chicken and the grilled juices contained bubbled out onto the plate.

Elijah chuckled. "Wait till you hear about The Olive Garden."

Bea snorted, and her hand shot to her face as she burst into a fit of giggles, which only made Elijah bloom into full laughter. He reached for the remote, and the screen glowed to life.

"What're we watching? I didn't peg you for a movie type of guy," Bea asked, turning her head to watch his reactions.

"*Gone with the Wind*. Had to rent it from the library."

Bea's heart swelled even larger in adoration for this scrumptious man. She tried desperately to contain her excitement at the news. "I thought twelve hours was too long?" she jabbed at him.

"Evelyn wanted to watch it." They both simultaneously looked down at Evelyn, who, sure enough, was eagerly watching the screen. Bea wondered if he'd secretly trained her to do that, or if she was a highly cultured individual.

Bea looked back up at Elijah, and caught him staring at her. They smiled at each other bashfully, their covers blown for the umpteenth time, before

settling into a long evening of watching the classic
movie.

~

An hour and a half later, right as Rhett was declaring
his love for Scarlett before leaving to join the Civil
War, Bea dared to chance a glance at Elijah. She
wanted to find out if he was as touched by the
moment as he should've been, since it was the most
epic of scenes.

Instead, he was completely asleep. His head was
leaned back on the couch, his mouth slightly opened
and emanating light snoring. Bea sat there and
watched him for a minute, enjoying her uncensored
opportunity to stare at this gorgeous, passed out
man. Bea glanced down at Evelyn, who had her head
propped up on Elijah's leg. With nothing
illuminating the room except the movie, Bea
couldn't tell if Evelyn's eyes were opened or closed,
but she was certainly breathing heavily for a dog.

Bea slowly scooted her table away and stood up,
careful not to wake the sleeping pair. She silently
collected both her and Elijah's plates and carried
them to the kitchen sink. She turned the kitchen
light off and slowly crept back into the living room,

and removed Elijah's tray from in front of him so he could stretch out if he needed to.

Bea searched around the room until she found an old quilt draped across the back of a recliner in the corner. She stealthily crept back to Elijah and laid the quilt over both him and Evelyn to keep them warm. She smiled at the uninhibited, peaceful expression across his face as he continued to snore lightly.

Bea stood to leave, and would have done so had a thought not crossed her mind.

She turned back around to Elijah, leaned down, and kissed his beautiful mouth while he slept.

Chapter Thirteen

"We may or may not have kissed," Bea said to Rhonda while she wiped down the counter.

"What do you mean, 'May or may not have?'" Rhonda said in her typical slow Southern drawl. She pulled the pen out from behind her ear. "Explain this to me. I feel like I'm goin' to need to take notes."

"Well, he was asleep. And have you ever seen a cupcake that looked so good, a chocolate cupcake, with fudge frosting and sprinkles, it looked so irresistible that you just had to lick it?" Bea closed her eyes and licked her lips.

"Sugar, are you tellin' me you just walked up and stuck your tongue on a sleepin' man? I have to say, I knew you were different, but I'm thoroughly entertained by your brand of crazy. Go on, what happened next? Jerry, you payin' attention?"

"Well, he'd fallen asleep, and he was so peaceful. And his lips were so pouty that I just, I just *had* to do *something*. Then, I kissed him."

"And?" Rhonda leaned on the counter. Her hair was neon blue this week, and it clashed horribly with the mustard stain on the collar of her uniform.

"And he kissed me back?" Bea shrugged her shoulders, not really knowing fully what to call it.

"He did what?!" Rhonda shot up so fast that her glasses slid off her nose and she had to catch them.

"Sort of. I mean, I'm not sure. He definitely kissed me back but I don't think he was awake. Maybe he was dream kissing?"

"Well, go on, what was it like? Jerry, take notes! I'm gettin' all bumfuddled with the details and I'm goin' to want to remember this one," Rhonda called over her shoulder through the window.

"It was like honey."

"Honey? You mean he had a sticky mouth?" Rhonda wrinkled up her nose.

"No, no. I mean like how it was. Slow and smooth and sweet."

"Oh, *honey*. Baptize me in sweet tea and call me Southern gospel!" Rhonda slapped her thigh. "I think I just peed myself a little bit. I can't decide if that's the creepiest or the ballsiest thing I've ever heard. You hearin' this, Jerry? You hear the cahooneys this one's got on her?"

Bea giggled. "I think it's pronounced ca-ho-nays. *Cajones.*"

"Whatever, sugar. Even a broken clock is right twice a day. I've got to say, though, I admire you. I really do. Sometimes you've got to do things you never thought you would. For example, every other night I take the fuzz buzzer to my neck and chin. You wouldn't understand this yet, but in the right light, I look like a Clydesdale. That's why I keep it slightly dim in here. Gotta keep the mystery alive for Jerry."

Bea automatically looked at Rhonda's neck. Rhonda stretched her head up proudly, like a turtle coming out of its shell.

"Nope, honey, last night was the night. No Clydesdales will be gallopin' through today's lunch rush!"

On Sunday, once again, Elijah showed up at church. And once again, he may or may not have asked Bea out.

On their third maybe-date the following Friday, Bea and Elijah awkwardly resumed their trek up the mountain to get more material for Bea's portfolio. It was much like the first time they'd come up here, except that Elijah had suggested that they start earlier, to catch more daylight.

There were ham and cheese sandwiches again, only this time with muenster instead of cheddar. *A slight, fancier upgrade to the previous version*, Elijah thought. He had also taken care to bring fresh fruit—grapes and strawberries—as well as a small cooler full of Mountain Dew exclusively for Bea.

Elijah was sitting on the flat rock, while Evelyn chased a butterfly. The only other sounds, besides the wind breezing past them, was Bea's gentle markings on her paper as she studied him.

"You got a boyfriend back at school?" Elijah had no idea where the question had come from. He already knew the answer from the way her doe eyes always stared at him. Googly-eyed, he'd heard his grandma say a time or two. If his grandma were still around, she'd say Bea resembled one of those goldfish with the eyes sticking out from each side of its head.

He'd had a pleasant dream last week, when he'd conked out during *Gone with the Wind.* Or at least, he'd thought it was a dream. When he'd woken up, there was a blanket draped across and tucked underneath both him and Evelyn, the movie credits were playing, and Bea was gone.

All week, he'd been thinking about it—whether or not she had actually kissed him. Whether or not he had actually kissed her back. In the dream, he had. In reality, he'd been wanting to. He knew she had guts, but he didn't know how far she'd put herself out there. Heavens knew how hard it was for him to put himself back out there.

"No, I don't. I'm an all or nothing type of woman. I never cared much for dating. It just feels so forced and expectations are too high and you're too nervous trying to be perfect and before you know it, you're more focused on whether or not the tomato skins got out of your teeth or if pepper is caught in your permanent retainer and if you're sitting up straight or not and if your Spanx are rolling down because you put them over the wrong fat rolls. It's just a whole thing."

"Wow. Sounds intense," was all Elijah could say. Maybe he'd been wrong about her after all. Maybe she wasn't really interested in him like that. He didn't think that was the case, but with women you never could tell. Just look at Ben and Tiffany.

The rest of their afternoon and evening had been mostly silent, and when they'd gotten back to the house, Bea had quickly helped him clean up the kitchen before practically running out the door before he could say anything.

Not that he would've said too much.

Chapter Fourteen

"Sugar, you said what?" Rhonda put her face in her hands. Her beehive was buttercup yellow this week.

"I don't know! It just came out! I word-vomited all over him and I don't even know what was happening."

"What'd he say in response to your shenanigans?" Rhonda rubbed her temples profusely, trying to squeeze her brain out.

"Well, it's Elijah … so, not much. He could've been quieter than usual, but then again, he's not really that chatty anyway. He said it sounded intense, and that was pretty much it. Then, I was so devastated with myself that I ran out and forgot my backpack with all my supplies in it. Maybe he'll bring it to church tomorrow, but I feel like he probably just hates me now."

"All right, listen, sugar. I hate to say this directly to your face, but I wouldn't be me if I didn't. Your love story is getting a little bit borin'. You've got what? A week left before you leave? Maybe two if you squeeze a clock? You've spent the whole summer swoonin' away for this weird fella with not a lot to show but some back and forth banter, combined with bleached spots on your britches and a soggy pillow full of tears."

Bea hung her head and tried not to cry as Rhonda continued, "You've got to keep the audience entertained, or else I'm about to subscribe to the telenovela channel to play in the kitchen just to keep things spicy for me and Jerry."

"Well, I've seen him the last three Fridays. And he has been to church the last two Sundays. I have no reason to think he won't be at church tomorrow, unless he's allergic to all my word vomit."

Rhonda shook her head sympathetically. "Darlin', I hate to break your heart, but this is Texas, where the cornbread's good and God is better. Just because a man goes to church, it's not a sure sign that he's tryin' to court you. Hopeful, sure, but you can't— and excuse my pun—take him to church on that fact alone. All's I'm sayin' is you better ramp up the sizzle, else your skillet's gettin' real cold."

~

"I wish his teeth were rotten. Or something. Anything." Bea huffed while she rearranged the carnations around the irises in the vase for the millionth time.

"Why is that?" Millie asked, grinning. After getting off work at the diner, Bea had randomly showed up at Millie's Florals. She said it was because she thought Millie needed help, but really, Millie knew it was because her granddaughter was restless and just trying to keep her mind occupied with other things besides Elijah Callahan.

"Because then I'd know he wasn't perfect and I could quit being blinded by his raw gorgeousness. If I could just find one flaw, then I could focus on that instead. Who is flawless? How is that even possible?" Bea squealed in disgust.

"Albuquerque St. Claire, you hush your mouth. Nobody on this earth is flawless. That poor man has had enough of a rough time in his life without you nitpicking to make him into something he's not."

"What happened? What rough life did he have?"

"He hasn't told you yet?"

"No, Grammy. He barely talks. Most of our conversations are one-sided, and always end up with me slurping the drool from my mouth and him laughing at me. That pretty much sums up our whole relationship."

"Well, maybe you need to drag it out of him then. Sit him down, tell him how you feel, and make him tell you how he feels and where you stand. You're fast running out of summer, Albuquerque."

"I can't do that. I mean, I kissed him. I did that. And that was amazing," Bea mused, as the carnations slumped over the side of the vase.

"Bea! You can't keep rearranging them! Now they're sad. Nobody wants sad flowers. Put them back in the cooler. I'll have to make them into boutonnieres." Millie sighed, and took them from her granddaughter before Bea could burst into tears for the eighth time since she'd shown up two hours ago.

"Carnations are sad anyway, because they're funeral flowers. They were destined to a life of sadness, just like me." Bea sobbed loudly.

"Quit feeling sorry for yourself and do something about it. And you better not go cleaning that man's house again. That's not what I'm talking about. You don't know how he feels because you never asked. Start asking."

"I can't do that. What if he hates me?"

"If he hated you, he wouldn't be spending time with you. And he certainly wouldn't cook his grandma's chicken for somebody he hates. They say you get three loves in your life, but most people are lucky if they get just one true one. Your grandpa was that for me, and I had to smack some sense into him to make him realize it too. Best thing I ever did, even though I had to get out of my comfort zone to do it."

"What'd you do? How'd you get him to notice you?" Bea pulled up a stool to the ribbon table and started wrapping the arrangements Millie had already finished.

"We'd been flirting off and on. Even though I had my heart set on him, he still hadn't asked me out. One day, I heard a rumor that he'd asked out Betty Burgess. The rage that I felt would've set all of Texas on fire. And remember, this was in the late Sixties. I put on the sassiest red dress I had, and did my hair and make-up real nice so he wouldn't know what hit him. Then, I marched over to the garage where he was working, and I cornered him in front of all his friends and co-workers."

"Then what happened?" Bea was leaning on the edge of her stool.

"His eyes were wide, and he thought something had happened to me. And it had. The fury of a thousand suns was coursing through my veins when I said as firmly as I could, 'I need to talk to you.'

"We walked outside, out of the immediate earshot of all of his people, even though they were all whistling at us. He asked me what was wrong and I'll never forget the concerned look in his eyes. Your grandpa had the most beautiful green eyes I've ever seen in my life. And black hair, mercy, he was a stunner. My knees were weak, and he took my hands into his grease-covered ones and asked me again what was wrong."

"Grandpa *was* a stunner; I remember your wedding pictures."

"Your dad is the spitting image of him. Then, I looked up at him and I said, 'James St. Claire. I heard

a rumor about you and I hope for my sake and yours
that it isn't true.'

"And he looked at me, his brows furrowed and
concerned like I was about to reveal the location of
the Ark of the Covenant. 'What rumor would that
be?' he said. I remember his face loosened and he
grinned at me, because he knew I was fired up about
something that was obviously not life and death,
even though to me, it absolutely was.

"And I said, 'James St. Claire, is it true that you
asked Betty Burgess to the movies? Is that true?'"

"Then what'd he say?"

"I wish you'd have known your grandpa. He was
always trying to get my feathers ruffled just to amuse
himself. This day was no different. He said, 'And
what if I did? What're you going to do about it?
She's a lot more friendly than you are.' He was still
holding my hands in his, and I felt my fists clench
into balls of anger. He caught my wrist midair before
I could slap his face. I was so mad I couldn't see
straight. Your grandpa was enjoying himself, though,
and he said, 'See? This is what I mean, Millicent.
Betty is a lot more passive.'

"I said, '*Passive?!* You want passive? I'll show you passive!' And before I could say another word, he pinned my arms behind my back and kissed me, right there in front of God and everybody at that garage. He held me up, his arms around my waist and his hands still clasping mine behind my back.

"'I don't want passive, Millie. I want passion.' He let me go and stepped back, and then he had to catch me because I immediately stumbled forward and back into his arms. 'You said you wanted to talk, but so far all you've done is a lot of screaming. Say what you came to say, Millie.'"

Bea slid off her stool and quickly grabbed the table to catch herself. "That's so romantic. Grandpa was a doozy, wasn't he? What'd you say?"

"I said, 'I don't want you to date Betty Burgess.' That was all that I could think to say. It came out as a whisper because I was so kerfuffled by how his lips had felt on mine, that I'd all but forgotten what my original purpose even was. Your grandpa chuckled and said, 'And why's that?'

"It turned out, he knew why. He hadn't asked out Betty at all. He told my friend to tell me that, to see how I'd react. Because one, we were both too shy to say anything, and two, he liked getting my feathers ruffled. He thought it was hilarious when I got mad at him.

"He asked me out to the movies, and two months later we were engaged. He used to always tell me he knew he was going to spend the rest of his life with me the minute I showed up at the garage in that red dress."

"I wish I remembered him. I bet he was really awesome," Bea said, lovingly.

"He was really awesome. He got to meet you, and he was so proud of you, Bea. He showed everyone your baby pictures all the time, even random strangers in the grocery store." Millie wiped a tear from her eye. "My point is, sometimes you have to do things you didn't know you were capable of doing in order to get the results you need."

Chapter Fifteen

"You've been awful quiet, Bea-utiful. What sort of scheming is going on up in that head of yours?" Millie asked as she locked the doors to her flower shop. By the time they'd gotten caught up with the floral arrangement orders, it was nearly 8 p.m.

"I was thinking you're right; I should go and talk to him. Plus, I may or may not have left my backpack in the kitchen before I ran out."

Millie nodded. "That sounds like a good idea. Just be careful. It's getting late. The bottom's going to drop out any minute now."

The wind pushed them to their car, as the smell of the storm enveloped them. Bea rolled her windows down to let the rain-scented air flow through.

By the time Bea got to Elijah's, it was nearly pitch black. She had driven slowly, because the rain was coming down on her in sheets. Now, it was calm, but the rumble of thunder rolled in the distance, over the mountains.

All of the lights in the house were off, and his truck was nowhere to be seen. Bea got out of her car and started walking up to the front porch, but stopped. Off in the distance, she heard a bark, and noticed a light bobbing up and down against a darkened shadow in the same location as the mine. Which didn't make sense, because Elijah had specifically told her to never go there. *What is he doing?*

Another bark sounded out, and Bea decided to go investigate and make sure that he was all right. She took out her phone and turned the flashlight on, and began the slow trek through the mud and fields of wetness, up the narrow path that led to the mine.

The mine was tucked away into the mountains, up a steep terrain. Bea took her time climbing each rock and root, trying to scout out the overgrown and long-forgotten path. It looked like no one had been using it, except maybe deer and rabbits. Bea silently prayed that she wouldn't encounter anything scarier than a cuddly forest creature just out for a bedtime stroll.

The entrance seemed to be faintly glowing as she got closer to it. She didn't hear or see Evelyn, and there were no signs of Elijah or his truck thus far. If he'd really wanted to, he could've gone off-roading and probably driven at least halfway to the mine before the mountain started sloping steadily upwards into a jagged forest landscape.

Then again, all of his cattle were in the valley down below, so maybe his truck was down there somewhere. Probably, a cow had wandered off. *Is that a thing? Or is that what sheep do?*

Bea tried to rationalize the growing sense of dread in her chest as she stopped to take a breath. Not unlike the first and second times she'd climbed the mountain with Elijah, Bea had discovered how out of shape she really was for someone her age.

The thunder rumbled a little bit closer, and Bea quickly hiked the rest of the way. The entrance was on a steep cliff, slippery with mud and moss. Bea straddled the side of the cave, holding her phone between her teeth with her arms and legs splayed out until she reached the opening.

The flashlight on her phone picked up something sparkly. Awe and wonder filled Bea's imagination as she neared the mine's entrance. She rounded the side, and saw that it was mostly just a dark, dirt-filled tunnel, with dusty wooden beams that looked at least a century old. An aged canteen, and a few rusted tin cans, littered the side.

Underneath the wooden supports, Bea found what had caught her attention earlier. A thin gold vein started at the entrance, thickening as the mine went deeper. It was the most beautiful, natural thing Bea had ever seen, short of Elijah Callahan himself. There were dozens of thinner veins scattered throughout the rock wall that seemed to be making the glow from earlier, but the one Bea was now following was growing wider. Her fingers traced the cold metal as she inched forward into the mine. A rumble in the distance sounded but she thought it was just the storm.

The old wooden support system beckoned her in further, its splinters disguising themselves in the shadows until another rumble sounded, this one much closer and much deeper, as if it were coming from the earth itself.

Bea's head slowly turned to her left, towards the darkness of the mine, her flashlight slowly following. She crept in further, expecting to see Evelyn dart out from the shadowy cavern at any moment.

"Elijah? Are you in here?" she whispered, but only the echo of her voice, combined with another low growl of earth, greeted her. A puff of dust fell from the wooden slat above her, and fear gripped Bea's stomach. She slowly turned back towards the entrance, not wanting to upset the mountain giant that lay dormant around her.

Another trickle of dust fell in front of her as the mountain shifted. A loud crack of thunder sounded throughout the tunnel, echoing so loud that Bea felt her bones dislocate. She turned to run, the crumbling mine fast on her heels. She slipped and tried to right herself, smacking against the cold, damp earth walls of the mine to propel herself further as she reached for the tunnel's entrance.

Just as the sprinkle of rain hit her face, Bea slipped and tumbled down the slope, the mine chasing after her all the way.

Chapter Sixteen

The thunder cracked directly overhead, and Elijah sat straight up in bed. Evelyn was nervously pawing at the door, trying desperately to get out.

"It's all right, it's just thunder," Elijah tried to comfort her, but she wasn't having it. She looked back at him with worried eyes and whined as she pawed the doorknob with more force, doing her best to turn it.

"All right, all right, I'm coming." Elijah got up, wincing at the pain that shot through his foot. Storms caused his old injuries to throb, and today had been particularly terrible. He'd sat in the shop all day waiting on his truck to be fixed, only for the mechanic to tell him to come back on Monday. Sitting still all day had made him hurt worse, and, combined with the storm, he was miserable.

If Evelyn had been a human, she would've been cursing at him for being a tortoise in the present moment. She brought one of his boots over, and dropped it in front of his feet.

"You don't need me to go outside with you." Elijah tried to scrub the sleep from his face while he watched Evelyn go and grab his other boot. It made a loud clunk on the floor as it fell. Evelyn put her paw on his good knee and, staring him down, barked loudly. She didn't bother to use her usual friendly bark, but instead, her demanding "This is what we're doing" bark.

"Fine, I got it. Calm down." Elijah stood and slipped on his jeans and a T-shirt over his boxers. Then slowly, he pulled on his boots, taking care to try and not anger his foot even more.

Evelyn ran back to the door and barked continuously, encouraging him to hurry up. Elijah opened the door and she raced down the stairs as fast as her furry legs could carry her. Lightning was cracking, illuminating the dark house like someone had plugged in a strobe light.

Elijah opened the door, and a gust of rain blew in. He shut his eyes, but when he opened them, he noticed Bea's car.

Evelyn was standing in the middle of the yard, barking madly and looking towards the mine. Bea was nowhere to be seen.

"Bea?" Elijah looked around the house from where he stood, but there were no lights on. There were no sounds except those of the storm and of Evelyn barking like she'd lost her mind. He squinted, peering into the empty driver's seat. Evelyn ran back up the stairs and chomped at his hand. *Listen to me, Dad!*

Finally, fully awake and concerned with his dog's erratic behavior, Elijah understood that Evelyn was trying to tell him something bad had happened. He grabbed his hat and walked out onto the porch. Evelyn raced back down the stairs and headed over to the side of the house, barking all the way for him to follow her.

Elijah heard the roar of the mine in the distance, and his stomach sank to the floor. He raced back into the house and grabbed his phone from the side table, and then burst out of the house.

Elijah was on the phone to Ben before he'd even made it off the porch. With Evelyn guiding, the pair raced up the path as best they could. The pain in his foot was the last thing on his mind. Silently, Elijah prayed that Bea was safe, and that the worst night of his life wasn't repeating itself.

~

By the time they reached the entrance, there was no entrance left to get to. The mountain had all but exploded into a massive heap of landslide, mud, and rocks.

Damn the night for being so dark. Elijah could barely see anything, and the light on his phone wasn't helping at all against the pouring rain that was now coming down, yet again, in curtains of thick liquid. His hat wasn't helping, either, because the wind was blowing half the rain sideways and directly into his face as he searched. Evelyn bounced around, barking at this tree and that. If Elijah could find Bea's footsteps, he could just track her and that would be that. Mother Nature wasn't going to help him out with this one, though. The ground squished beneath him as his eyes darted frantically to anything that might resemble anything.

"Bea! Bea! Can you hear me?" Elijah yelled at the top of his lungs, challenging the thunder on who could be louder. If Man vs. Thunder were a reality show, the intro credits would be Elijah roaring at the sky and the sky roaring back.

He was nauseous with worry, praying that she wasn't even here. Maybe she was at the pond, playing with the frogs. That would be a Bea thing to do. But then Evelyn wouldn't be freaking out if nothing was wrong.

Elijah scoured the slides of mud, looking for anything he could find, any sign of Bea. He couldn't go to the mine, there was no mine left to go to. It was completely caved in. He swore out loud for not having blown it up sooner, and putting everyone out of their misery. The mine had been nothing but a death trap since it had opened, cursing the entire Callahan lands.

~

Bea was fast fading in and out of consciousness. Her body didn't feel great, but her head was throbbing terribly. She was sore, wet, and cold. And gross. Wherever this was, it felt dirty and soggy, like she was laying on the bottom of a swamp.

Bea's eyes blinked open slightly. An old man was standing over her, smiling thoughtfully.

"Sshhh, you're fine. I've got you," the man whispered. He was oddly clean, for being in a landslide, and he emitted a pale glow. It was strange to her that even in the nighttime, and even though rain and grit were caking her eyes, he was clearly visible. He smiled at her again, and patted her head. His touch was cool and soothing. Bea smiled back weakly, before her consciousness betrayed her trust. The last thing she heard before she blacked out was, "She's over here!"

At the sound of an old man's voice, Evelyn and Elijah's heads both snapped up in the direction of a tree about thirty yards away. Leaving Elijah's side, Evelyn raced towards the sound. Upon finding Bea, she began to bounce up and down and bark even more wildly than before. Elijah hobbled and crawled over the muddled terrain until he collapsed at Bea's side.

  Evelyn was doing her best to lick Bea awake, but Bea wasn't responding. Her body was halfway covered in mud and rocks, and her breathing was shallow at best from what Elijah could tell with his phone light. He pushed as much of the earth off of her as he could, and pulled her from under the rest of it. Her lifeless body collapsed against him as he fell backwards. He cradled her in his arms, brushing the hair back from her face as he repeated her name over and over.

"Bea, please wake up. Please, please wake up." Her eyes fluttered, but just barely.

Elijah tried a different approach. "Albuquerque, this is not a great time to be stubborn right now. You can prove whatever point you're going for later. I need you to wake up." Still nothing.

Evelyn licked Bea's limp hands, trying to get a response. Then, because he knew it was what she would want, and what he wanted, too, Elijah kissed her lips. Tears fell from his eyes when it had no effect.

"I'm sorry, Bea. I'm sorry for everything," he whispered into her ear. Elijah stood up, and lifted her into his arms. With Evelyn leading the way and nothing illuminating his path except his dying phone and the lightning, Elijah carried Bea slowly back down the mountain, taking care not to stumble or fall with his delicate cargo. In the distance, blue lights pulled up to the Callahan ranch.

Chapter Seventeen

Rhonda burst through the doors of the ER wearing fuzzy pink house shoes and a pink flamingo muumuu. "Ben! Benjamin! I'm here! I've arrived!"

Millie shot up from her chair in the waiting room, pulling her flannel robe tight around her for extra defense. "What're you doing here, you old coot? Nobody in this facility spoke your name, let alone bothered to call you."

"I heard his siren song on the scanner. Usually, I just let his voice put me to sleep, but then he mentioned our two star-crossed lovers and I thought I'd come down here to assist him."

"There's no assisting you can do for Ben or anyone else in this town. Stick to French fries and grease patties," Violet snapped at Rhonda. She stood about a foot taller, and looked much more practical and level-headed in her matching blue silk pajama set and tennis shoes.

"Nobody asked you, Vomit," Rhonda retorted.

"That's real mature, Rancid. In fact, I was called for moral support. You're just a pain in everyone's a—"

"Ladies, calm down." Ben walked into the room. "Rhonda, step away from everybody who has a right to be here."

"*I* have a right to be here, Benji. The heart wants what the heart wants."

"Keep pushing me and I'll have you committed. Go home, Rhonda," Ben snapped in an unfriendly tone. He stared her down with his Carolina blue eyes and watched her wither right in front of him. But Rhonda always gets the last word.

"Oh, Benji, I love it when you get all serious with me," she said, as she shook her chest at him. "It gets me all hot and bothered."

"Unbelievable," Violet groaned loudly. "People like her are what's wrong in this world."

"Any news yet?" Ben asked, turning to Millie when Rhonda had finally—after a painfully slow walk—strutted back out the door. He'd been in the room with Elijah, who'd been checked out by the doctor just to make sure he hadn't reinjured his foot in anyway.

By the time Elijah had gotten to Ben's police car, he was limping worse than normal. He had collapsed against the vehicle, as Ben rushed forward to take Bea from him. Ben had carefully placed her in the back of the car before propping Elijah on his shoulder and helping him hobble to the passenger's seat.

"She's stable. The doctor said it looks like a minor concussion, sprained wrists, and a lot of bruises and scrapes. He said she's really, really lucky, considering she effectually surfed half a mountain. If Elijah hadn't gotten there, I don't know …" Millie's eyes welled up with tears and she sobbed loudly. Violet stood up and moved to stand by her best friend in silent support, armed with a half-full box of tissues.

Elijah hobbled through the double doors of the ER, on crutches. As soon as Millie saw him, she ran and flung herself into him, nearly causing him to topple over. She put her hands on his face and brushed his beard down repeatedly.

"You beautiful boy, you beautiful, sweet boy. If you hadn't been there, my Bea, she could've—"

Elijah wrapped an arm around her, shifting half his body weight to one crutch. "It's all right, ma'am. Wasn't really me, though. It was Evelyn. She did all the hard work," he said with a smile, trying to lighten the mood of the room.

"What'd the X-rays say?" Ben asked.

"Same thing they always say. Nothing new, just really bad weather today." He looked back at Millie, trying not to show his own state of emotions. "How is she?"

Millie wiped the tears from her eyes with the sleeve of her robe. Then she patted his chest. "I think you should go sit with her. She needs you, Elijah."

~

Elijah tried not to make any sound that might disturb the serenity around her. She'd come out pretty banged up, but overall, she was fine. It could've been a lot worse.

It could've been a lot better, too. Elijah sighed as he sat down in the chair beside her hospital bed. Her chest slowly rose and fell, keeping time with the hospital machines. If he'd pushed her out of his house and out of his life that day, none of this would've happened.

She had been like an adorable beam of joy, though. Bright and happy and there to slice through his guarded exterior. If she hadn't been so cute when she set her mind to do something, if her face didn't have that determined look when she was serious, he might've kept his wits about him.

It hadn't helped that Evelyn had immediately taken a liking to her, too.

Elijah wet a paper towel and gently wiped some of the crusted mud from Bea's forehead. He bet it was the mountain spirits, or his grandpa. Maybe his grandpa had finally decided to get back at him by taking it out on the woman he—

Bea's eyes fluttered. He leaned forward a little, propping his forearms on the edge of her bed and stretching his leg out to the side as far as he could.

"You shouldn't have come here. You should've stayed in Austin. All the rumors … everything you heard is true. I'm a murderer," Elijah whispered.

He waited for her to respond, to tell him he was being ridiculous and that she wasn't afraid of a man who had a ponytail, or a man who fed his dog chicken and dumplings on her birthday. Some Bea-ism she would come up with, that would make him feel like less of a monster. If just for a minute.

"I need to tell you, I'm cursed. Not just by the ghosts that nearly got you tonight." The steady beep of the heart monitor was Bea's only conversational response.

Elijah ran a hand through his damp, dirty hair, and sighed. "I killed my mama," he whispered. He waited for her response before he continued.

"On the night I was born. The doctor said it was an aneurysm, that it couldn't have been predicted or prevented. But I know it was me, because I killed everyone else."

Bea still didn't move.

"My daddy died when I was five, from liver failure and a broken heart."

He readjusted in his chair, trying to find a position that didn't grate on his foot and make it ache.

"My grandparents raised me, but they blamed me for killing their daughter. I know they did. They didn't say it, but I saw it every day in their eyes. Every time they looked at me, they saw their daughter's reflection."

Bea's eyes fluttered again, but she didn't move otherwise. Behind Elijah, the steady beep and line of the heart monitor gently increased.

Elijah leaned forward and kissed her forehead. Then he took her hands in his and kissed them, brushing his lips against the scrapes and cuts on her knuckles and palms from where she'd fought for her life just hours earlier.

"I lost my head with you, Bea. I'm supposed to stay away from people. I have to. People never want me around anyway, because they don't want the curse. I don't blame them. I just keep to myself."

He waited a few minutes to see if she would respond to anything he'd said, or to the sound of his voice at all.

"You asked me once why I talk to chickens. It's easier to talk to animals in general. They don't expect anything from you, besides basic needs. Food, shelter, like a Maslow's hierarchy of needs sort of deal. They don't want the other stuff, the hard stuff. I couldn't give it to them if they did.

"When I was twelve, my grandma died. We were in the car, coming back from the grocery store. It was raining hard, a lot like it was tonight. I was singing along with the radio, too loud. She told me to quit because I was distracting her concentration.

"I'll never forget the moment she turned to look at me. She was laughing, even though she was mad. I was singing in a stupid voice, and she was tickled even though she was trying to be serious. She thought she'd stopped at the stop sign. If I hadn't been trying to make her laugh, she would've known she hadn't."

Elijah sobbed, and hid his face with his hands. No living person had seen him cry except Ben, and he wasn't about to change that fact. He dried his tears before he continued.

"Bea, I told you to stay away from the mine." Elijah sighed and crossed his forearms on the bed, then laid his head down against them. At the response of the bed shifting with his slight movement, the heart monitor behind him paced unnoticeably faster.

He lifted his head to watch her sleep. "The night my grandpa died, we were up in the mine. He had this wild notion that if he could find enough nuggets, he could send me to a better college. Irony was, I already had a football scholarship. His dream was that I become a Gold Digger across town. I was never good enough to make it to them, or to any other NFL team, but it would at least get me a degree."

Elijah chuckled to himself. "Bet you didn't see that one coming, huh? One night, we're up in the mine, way down deep. Twice as deep as what you saw. Ben was there, too, but he'd gone back to the house to get more batteries for our headlamps. My grandpa always said the mine was haunted, that it had killed the first prospectors who had opened it, and had claimed even more lives since.

"I'd never seen a ghost, and you of all people know how rumors and old wives' tales can be. When he said the spirits were getting angry, I ignored him and kept digging." Elijah went silent for several minutes.

With his voice in a hushed whisper, he resumed his story. "It was my fault we stayed as long as we did. Next thing I know, the earth is falling out from under me. My grandpa shoved me hard towards the entrance as the mine collapsed on him. I tripped and fell, and it broke my leg and shattered all the bones in my foot and ankle in the process."

He was sobbing, and trying to wipe the tears away with the edge of the hospital blanket that lay across Bea. "I couldn't even see him. I yelled for him, tried to dig him out, but there was just so much. Ben dragged me outside to safety, and then went and called 911."

Elijah took Bea's hands in his, and kissed them again. "What I'm trying to say is that you can't be here, Bea. You need to leave. It was a nice summer, but it's over now. Go back to where you belong."

He grabbed his crutches and stood up to leave the room.

When the door shut behind him, a silent tear rolled down Bea's cheek.

Chapter Eighteen

Bea slowly and painfully packed her backpack with all of her drawing supplies. Elijah had dropped it off at some point during the three days she'd been in the hospital. Her wrists were bandaged, and she wore giant darkened glasses to help keep her head from pounding. Physically, she was feeling better every day.

Emotionally was a different story entirely. Bea was depressed and had cried all the time since leaving the hospital, which the doctor said could be another side effect from her concussion. It was supposed to gradually fade as she healed, but Bea knew otherwise.

Bea had woken up to see Elijah's head lying beside her, his voice unsteadily telling her how he'd lost his grandparents. She had the sense that he'd told her more, but she hadn't woken up in time to hear it. She'd faded in and out, but she desperately tried to cling on to every word he was openly telling her when he thought she wasn't listening to him.

The last words, she'd definitely heard. Loud and clear.

They'd had fun, but now it was over.

She didn't belong in Goodwater Ranch.

Bea St. Claire didn't belong with Elijah Callahan.

When Millie pushed the door open to her bedroom, Bea was crying in the middle of the floor, again.

"Honey, the doctor said this phase will pass. I brought you some lemonade and Tylenol just in case." She leaned down to hand her granddaughter a glass of ice-cold lemonade. Bea held her palm up as Millie dropped two pills into it.

"It's not that. It's … what do I do now?" Giant tears rolled down her cheeks beneath her glasses.

"You go back to school is what you do. You keep being the fabulous you that you were meant to be."

"But Elijah doesn't want me."

"Honey, that boy doesn't know what he wants. You're the best thing that's ever happened to him. He may talk slow, but he's not stupid. Sooner or later, he'll realize it and come around. And if he doesn't, and someone better comes along in the meantime, then it was never meant to be in the first place. What did you learn from this whole summer?"

"That I'll never love again." Bea took a long hard gulp of lemonade, and nearly choked herself.

"Wrong. You learned that you've got to protect yourself better. The Lord said you've got to guard your heart. You can't go throwing it around at every man who comes along, thinking he'll devote his life to you just because you pledged your undying devotion to him. That's not how it works. You've got to shield yourself until the right man *does* come along."

"I don't think I'll know when it's right."

"Well, how about this? How about you ask for something? Something specific, so that when he's standing right in front of you, you'll know he's yours."

Bea wiped her eyes beneath her glasses and nodded. "I want him to tell me that he's mine. No room for error."

"OK, well, that may be reaching a little too high, but the good Lord can and will provide. I have no doubts about that."

She looked at Bea's art supplies. "Did you get your portfolio finished?"

"I did, but I'm going to scrap it and start over. I think I'll just stick to landscapes for a while."

Millie nodded. "There never was a problem that a good mountain range painting couldn't solve."

Chapter Nineteen

On the first Thursday of September, Ben showed up precisely on time at the Callahan ranch. It had been exactly three weeks since Bea had left town.

Evelyn came out to greet him, as was her usual custom, except that this time she whimpered at him.

"What is it, girl? Are you OK?" Ben reached behind him to get the groceries from the backseat. Evelyn barked, and then ran back up to the porch, eagerly awaiting Ben to follow her. When he opened the door, she waited for him to walk through first before she followed after.

"Oh, I see, you couldn't call the cops so you waited until they came to you." Ben ran a hand through his hair, making himself appear as frazzled as Evelyn felt. He let out a sigh as he looked around worriedly.

The banister and railing on the staircase were broken, and busted splinters of wood lay up and down the hallway. A steady series of holes lined the sheetrock, where it looked like someone, definitely Elijah, had taken out his frustrations.

"Elijah!" Ben called out.

"Be down in a minute," a voice from upstairs called back.

Ben looked around at the mess before looking at Evelyn. She was giving him her saddest dog eyes while trying to communicate with him telepathically. *Yeah, it's been bad.*

Elijah hobbled down the stairs, closer to the wall side, since there was no railing. Ben noticed the wall also displayed a nice series of holes.

"Holy crap on a cracker, what happened?" Ben watched his friend take the stairs slowly, taking care to step around the shards of wood and chunks of sheetrock instead of cleaning them up. His fists were bandaged, and spots of blood were soaking through.

"Got mad is all," Elijah said flatly.

"I see that. Looks more like somebody broke in and tried to murder your house."

Elijah walked past him and headed towards the kitchen, not bothering to humor Ben.

Evelyn waited for Ben to start walking before she followed. "Want to talk about it? You're scaring your dog half to death."

"Just hates loud noises," Elijah muttered, as he turned to walk into the kitchen.

Ben propped up against the kitchen door frame and crossed his arms. The bag of groceries dangled from his fist. "So, we're back to Two-Word Elijah now? And here I thought you were finally crawling out of your shell."

If his friend wasn't going to talk, he was going to have to make him talk. "Your girl isn't going to appreciate this one bit, after all the hard work she did."

Elijah slammed the cutting board down on the counter. "She's not my girl."

"Well, maybe not anymore. But she was, and you'd better fix it before she gets back or else she's gonna be piiiiissssssed." Ben's voice went higher just to grate on Elijah's nerves.

Elijah slammed the refrigerator door, and what sounded like one of the shelves clattered inside like it had fallen off. "She's not my girl."

"And who's fault is that? Certainly not Evelyn's." Evelyn wagged her tail as Ben scratched her behind her ears. "She did everything her little dog heart could possibly do, but sometimes good dogs happen to dumb men." He said the last sentence with a baby voice, while pinching both of her cheeks. Evelyn just blinked at him and wagged her tail slowly, because she was a good girl.

Elijah stopped and turned around to face Ben. "You done yet, or do you need to leave?" he growled.

Ben threw his hands up in defeat. "Fine, fine. Don't listen to my two cents' worth. Just glad you realize what a mistake you made."

Elijah raised his head and his gaze to challenge Ben.

"I'm done. Moving on." Ben shook the bag of groceries like a white flag of surrender. "I got a pork loin this time."

~

It was the Sunday before Thanksgiving, the day the church's annual big potluck was held. It was really no different than all of the other potlucks, except that Preacher Dan traditionally deep-fried about five turkeys, and Millie made about four large roasting pans of her famous tetrazzini.

And, every year, despite their best intentions, the evening service was always canceled due to everyone—including Preacher Dan himself—passing out from a food coma.

Elijah had come to every Sunday church service and corresponding potluck since Bea had left. He never much participated, but, since it was Thanksgiving, he'd gone the extra mile and tried to make devilled eggs. They weren't exactly picture perfect, but they still tasted great. He figured that's what really counted.

Elijah and Ben were quietly eating in the corner of the community building and minding their own business when they heard an awful ruckus coming from the drink table that sounded like a bunch of chattering hens.

The gaggle of resident busybodies, Rhonda along with her two best friends Carmilla McNulty and Karen Cutter among them, were standing directly in Millie and Violet's path. They were loudly whispering and staring at the two determined women.

Millie bumped Karen away rudely with her hip as she walked by. "Move over, KAREN," Millie screamed loudly. "Have some respect for an old woman and get out of my way." She weaved through the crowd, making an obvious beeline straight towards Elijah and Ben.

"Uh oh," Ben whispered. Both of the grown men were suddenly terrified of the incoming confrontation. She was glaring at Elijah as she walked, and he tried to ignore her by staring down at his plate.

By now, everyone else in the community hall had turned to listen to the commotion. Millie turned around again to confront the blatant gossiping behind her back. Karen and Rhonda's eyes grew wide at the realization that they were being singled out.

Millie bared her teeth and spoke slowly, "Mind your own business, Rhonda. Ain't nothin' to see here but some friends eating. Last I checked, all are welcome in the Lord's house, so why don't you darn well start acting like it?"

She slammed her plate down and corn nuggets scattered off, erupting away like cockroaches when the lights turned on. Millie quickly picked them all back up and balanced them on the side of her plate.

Despite his scraggly beard, she could tell Elijah was grinning at her, a twinkle in his eyes. "How you doing, honey? You all right? You get enough to eat?"

"Yes, ma'am, for now." His plate was piled high with her tetrazzini.

Millie waved her fork towards it in a circular motion, like she was stirring her cauldron. "I like to grace them with its presence every so often. The Lord says you should be generous and all, and anytime Dora plans this, that means she's gonna fix one of them horrendous aspics that no one ever touches, and then she brags about it. Look at it up there, jiggling like it's in a night club. Nobody's even walked to that end of the table because they're afraid."

Elijah snickered and started eating again. Millie focused her attention on Ben. "No Tiffany?"

Ben had been trying to remain invisible by staying focused hard on the task at hand. Being singled out caused him to choke on a noodle. "She's working."

"Mm-hhhhmm," Violet murmured, acknowledging all that was unsaid.

"Well anyway, honey, I make it a habit to mind my own business," Millie said loudly, turning once again to acknowledge the eyes that were boring a hole in her back. "That's right, I sit with *all* the hot guys. Jealous much, you old hag? I might get *Aawwwfissa*," she hung on the word, enunciating it until it was in an irreversibly deep Southern drawl to mock Rhonda, "Camden here to handcuff me just to spite you."

"Millie!" Ben fussed, his cheeks pinking at her words.

"Whatever, honey. Everybody knows she's got a mad crush on you. She's old enough to be your grandmother."

"So are you, Millie," Ben said delicately, unsure of hurting her feelings on the subject.

"Yes, sugar, but the difference between us is I'm still sexy and she's not."

"And you're extremely tolerable," Ben added.

"I will take that as a compliment."

"It was meant to be, ma'am." His eyes reverted back down to his plate, trying to return to invisibility mode.

"Anyway, why did I come over here?" She looked at Violet, who pointedly looked at Elijah.

"Oh, yes, that was it. Elijah. Sweetheart. I've got some things to say and I need you to listen up."

Ben snickered while Elijah shifted uncomfortably in his seat before Millie continued, "You didn't start coming to church until my granddaughter was here, and judging from everything I know and have gathered, I'm going to go ahead and venture to not mind my own business, just this once. You've been moping around here every weekend since she left. You're a smart man, but right now you seem to have the emotional IQ of a potato chip."

Ben nearly choked on his mashed potatoes while she continued, "Facts are facts. So, I'm going to help you out. If you feel anything for her, truly, and you don't just love her company, you need to tell her."

Elijah looked at her like a deer in headlights.

"That's right, I said what I said. You knew it was coming. Don't act so surprised. I've given you all summer until now to figure it out on your own, and you haven't."

Elijah remained silent. Millie huffed loudly in frustration. "Benjamin, you better hold me back. No, scratch that, you better call the force, because you won't be able to contain me once I light into this boy. Elijah, I ought to yank a knot in your tail so tight they'll have to make you a marionette puppet just to help you walk at all."

She slammed her fist down on the table, and a corn nugget hopped off her plate. "How dare you go and break my granddaughter's heart like that. Are you emotionally crippled or romantically challenged? Women aren't hard to figure out, dear. Some need you to show, some need you to tell. The way you figure that out is to see how they treat you."

Millie propped her elbows on the table and leaned forward. "Here's a lesson for the both of you about women. If we want your attention, we sometimes overexert ourselves to make you notice. For this example, I will use 'cleaning up one-hundred years of Callahan clutter in three months.' Did you notice her? Sure seems like it. Did you say anything? No, you didn't, because she still calls me to ask how you are. Every time I talk to my granddaughter on the phone, I have to give her a status update about you. She worries about you; she cares about you. Above her own self, she wants to make sure that you are doing all right." Millie groaned and pulled the skin on her face down as she rolled her eyes in frustration.

"My granddaughter pulled out all the tricks to make you notice her, and as far as I'm tellin', every one of them worked. Now you need to pay it back to her in the same way, with a big-grand-gesture declaration of your devoted love. Ya'll need somebody to draw out roadmaps to see what's right in front of you, and it's downright exhausting."

Elijah just stared at her, confused, as she continued talking. Millie waved her hands in the air. "Whatever. Anyway, here's my problem. I gave you all the time in the world to figure this out for yourself, but just this week she informed me that she's had several dates with some idiot in one of her classes who's not even worth the price of her shoes. Yet, she still asks about you. And you're still here at church every Sunday wandering around all aimless and pitiful, like one of those neglected puppy commercials.

"So, here I am. It's time I step in because I am tired of this mess. I will not let you or her or that bozo she's dating ruin Thanksgiving. I really like you, Callahan. I'm telling you now, you should tell her how you feel. Go to her, and tell her. That's an order."

She swirled her finger around in a circle at him. "And clean that tumbleweed off your face. That's also an order. Let everybody else see you the way she sees you, and maybe they'd shut the hell up once and for all."

The four of them ate in silence until Ben was so uncomfortable that he excused himself. "Violet, if you would kindly leave us. I need to talk to this young man alone," Millie said, her voice returning to her usual pleasant tones. Violet nodded, and made her way over to the dessert table.

"I'm not good for her, ma'am," Elijah whispered.

"Boy, you've been talking to chickens for too long. You're the best thing that's ever happened to her. You changed her life, and she changed yours."

"I'm damaged. She's not safe with me," Elijah whispered.

"I'm not talking about your foot. She wouldn't give two flying figs if you were missing a whole leg. She's

in love with your spirit," Millie said, her voice trying
to remain kind towards him.

She sighed, and reached across the table to pat his
hand. "Son, I know you've got spiderwebs up there
in that hat of yours, but we all do. And I know you
blame yourself for what happened at the mine, but I
knew your grandpa really well. Where do you think
he got those maple trees from all those years ago?
I'm telling you, and you better listen to me, he was
prouder of you than anything else in his life.
Anybody who's got a lick of sense knows you did
the best you could to save him, and you paid for it
with a limp for the rest of your life.

"Elijah, don't feel ashamed of who you are. And
don't be afraid of letting someone into your heart.
Especially my granddaughter. And just so you know,
she's staying on campus through the holidays. By
herself, too, except for meals with her parents. And
she's awfully lonely and heartbroken and trying to fill
the void you left by dating some guy with dumbo
ears. Can you imagine?"

Just to drive the point home, in case he hadn't
figured it out, she said, "And it's your fault. I think
maybe you should go see her. Maybe you should
kick your demons in the crotch, or better yet, let her

help you kick them. Nobody should go through their days alone when beautiful, life-changing love is right in front of them. Are you hearing me or do I need to escort you myself?"

"I'll kill her," Elijah muttered under his breath.

"I don't feel like you've been paying attention to anything I've said. The only part of you that's actually killing her is your silence about how you really feel."

Elijah nodded slowly, contemplating.

"You think you've got a ghost problem on that ranch now? If you don't make it right, just wait till I die. You'll never hear the end of it. Your devilled eggs taste great, though," Millie added, just for good measure.

Chapter Twenty

Bea really didn't even like Jeff that much. He was hot, and he was funny. That was about it. By all accounts, he was a complete meathead. He'd been in one of her art classes, because he thought it would be an easy credit. "How hard is it to throw some color on some paper?" he'd said.

"Paint on canvas, is the phrase you were trying to say," Bea had snapped, which had delighted Jeff for whatever reason. For the last month, they'd had coffee together and talked about stupid school stuff nearly every day after class.

Last week, they'd gone to dinner and a movie. Dinner had been decent, but not exciting. She'd ordered grilled chicken at a barbecue restaurant, and spent the whole time thinking how much better Elijah would've cooked it. For dessert, they'd split a piece of pecan pie, which tasted more like corn syrup and flour than anything.

Later, Bea honestly couldn't even remember the name of the movie. Jeff had chosen it, without consulting her, because he said she needed to be cultured. It was some action flick starring whatever big action star of the moment. Bea drank extra caffeine and tried to desperately focus on not falling asleep due to the lack of a plotline.

Jeff was on the baseball team, which she liked. Not that she knew anything about baseball at all, but he was tall and strong and athletic-looking. She liked that about him, that physically he was as tall and as broad as Elijah. Sometimes she even pretended she was walking across campus with Elijah, until Jeff opened his mouth and ruined the illusion.

Right before Thanksgiving break, he'd told her he was going home and wanted to know if she wanted to meet his parents. Thus ruining the illusion, again.

"Look, Jeff. It's nothing personal, but this isn't going anywhere."

He'd acted like he was heartbroken. "I thought you had a good time."

"I did, but like, you've already asked me to meet your parents. Dude, it's been a month. You know nothing about me, we have nothing in common.

Let's call this what it was, which was just a bunch of coffee dates, and move on. I don't want to spend the holidays feeling guilty or leading you on when you clearly think there's more here than there is. There's not."

Bea felt bad for being a little harsh with him, but she didn't have the heart to put into a relationship. Any relationship. She'd even gotten an aloe plant when school started back up, which had already rotted and died from overwatering and being over-nurtured. She betted if she got an air plant, she'd even kill it from breathing literal air on it too much. If that's even how it worked.

~

The Monday before Thanksgiving, it was gray and gloomy outside. The only things on campus that were open were the library and the cafeteria, which was only halfway stocked with grab-and-go items for the sad stragglers who had nowhere to go. Bea selected a pre-packaged chicken salad sandwich—which she hoped wouldn't give her stomach issues later on—a cream cheese Danish, and a Mountain Dew before checking out and heading outside.

Bea only stayed on campus because she wanted to immerse herself in the full college experience. That, and parking was a nightmare.

Her parents lived about forty minutes away. She'd planned to go home on Wednesday and come back Thursday night. Until then, Bea would be putting the final touches on the senior portfolio that she'd stressed herself to do. After she threw herself the weekly pity party, of course.

Bea had decided to dress cute this morning, if only to cheer herself up. She'd put on her favorite pair of boots, which were brown, with buttons and three-inch heels, like a steampunk princess would wear. She paired them with purple leggings and a cream sweater, along with her favorite tan trench coat that came down to her knees. It was a bit chilly outside, so she left her hair down to flow around her shoulders.

There was a happy couple walking across the grounds opposite from her, their laughter disappearing through the door as they entered the library. Bea found her favorite bench, beneath a massive oak tree, and sat down.

She unwrapped her sandwich, which was cold and gooey and not a great selection in the equally cold weather. Bea frowned as she picked off the slimy lettuce that looked more like wilted spinach than romaine. She tossed it behind her, hearing the gentle *plop* as it landed against the tree bark.

Bea bit into the remaining sandwich, and promptly gagged. The bread was as soggy as the lettuce, and only held the appearance of still being bread. In reality, it squished on impact and melded with the chicken salad in the middle to form a single substance. Bea rewrapped the sandwich in the plastic wrap it had come in.

Then, hoping for better luck with the cream cheese Danish, she gently unwrapped it and licked off the cream cheese that had stuck to the plastic. It wasn't great, but it was good enough. Her stomach growled as she took the first bite, and then it slipped from her fingertips.

Bea watched as the Danish fell in slow motion, bouncing down her lap and leaving a spot of cream cheese on her boot before falling to the ground.

With her mouth open in disbelief, Bea stared at the discombobulated dessert as giant tears formed in her eyes.

"This is so stupid. Everything is so stupid," she said to no one in particular. A cold gust of wind blew through the campus, chilling her tears against her skin.

Bea closed her eyes and lifted her face up to the sky. "God, why is everything so stupid? I really just, like, I can't deal with this today."

Winter clouds rolled overhead. It wasn't supposed to rain, but it was cold enough that she should probably go back indoors. She just didn't feel like it.

"God, my heart hurts. My soul hurts, I just ache. I can't deal with all this. I just feel like the world is sitting on my chest. And I know, *I know*, you don't have to say it. A broken heart isn't really a big deal in the grand scheme of things, there are a lot of worse problems to have, and I'm really fortunate. But God, it just hurts so bad. Everything is so stupid, and I'm hungry, and I'm tired. I'm just tired."

Tears rolled down her cheeks and bounced off her jacket, soaking into her leggings while Bea kept her eyes closed. In the distance, she heard a dog bark, and her thoughts immediately shifted to Evelyn.

How do dogs know what you're feeling? How can you not even speak the same language as dogs and cats but you understand them better than any human? Now she finally understood what Elijah had meant about the chickens. Really, truly understood.

A whoosh and a chomp at her feet caused Bea to open her eyes and look down. A black and white border collie sat in front of her. There was no Danish on the ground.

The dog placed her paw on Bea's leg, and Bea slid down to the ground and wrapped her arms around her. She squeezed her eyes closed, forcing out all the stray tears that had held themselves back.

Whether it was an angel or Evelyn herself, Bea didn't know. She was just glad she was here. "Hey, girl, what're you doing here?" Bea buried her face in the dog's neck, and Evelyn thumped her tail in response.

Behind her, Bea heard the steady and slow gait that was trademark Elijah Callahan. She dared not turn around, though, for fear that her heart would break into an unsalvageable mess. She squeezed Evelyn harder, trying to hold on to the moment.

The footsteps stopped behind her on the sidewalk, and the bench creaked from a settling weight.

Bea wiped the tears from her eyes, again, and stood up, still afraid to look in his direction to see if he was real or not. She sat down on the bench beside him, daring to glance at the ground and see his cowboy boots to determine if he, in fact, was really beside her.

"Why're you crying?" Elijah asked, which made Bea start crying even more. Evelyn moved and laid her head in Bea's lap to comfort her.

"Bad day," Bea sobbed.

"What happened?"

"Nothing. I'm just older and wiser now, and I know the ways of the world." She scratched Evelyn's ears absent-mindedly.

"Is that so? Where's your boyfriend?"

"I broke up with him."

"Did he hurt you? Is that what's wrong?" Elijah shifted forward, eagerly awaiting her response.

"No, Elijah. I wouldn't even really classify him as a friend. He was just somebody who was just there, which wasn't fair to him."

"Somebody who was just there," he repeated.

"Yeah, like when you're lonely and you need someone, and someone shows up. He was just there."

They sat there, both staring at the ground. Bea still hadn't dared to look up at his beautiful face, because she knew she would shatter.

"What're you doing here?" she asked after a minute.

"Heard you dropped your Danish," he said, and Bea smiled the cheesiest grin despite herself. They both laughed. Evelyn wagged her tail, happy that the mood had lightened at least a little bit.

Bea dared to look at his face, and her heart stopped. Her eyes widened as large as tire rims at the vision beside her. He was wearing his cowboy hat, with his long hair pulled back in a ponytail beneath it, but also … "You shaved," she whispered.

Elijah's long beard was now a closely trimmed scruff, fully outlining his chiseled jaw and showing off the most perfect pink lips that Bea had only dreamed of seeing before now. He grinned, judging from her reaction that he'd completely upended her.

"You hungry?" Elijah asked. He stood up and held his hand out to her.

"Famished," Bea said, and placed her hand in his.

Chapter Twenty-One

"How's the farm?" Bea asked, as she swirled Dan Dan noodles around her chopsticks.

"The *ranch* is fine. How are you doing that?" Elijah asked, while using a fork to eat his orange chicken.

"I don't know, I just do it. Balance. It's easier with noodles than with rice. What's the difference?" She slurped a big mouthful.

"Farm is field and dairy, ranch is livestock."

"OK, how're the cows?" Bea stabbed a piece of pork with one of the sticks.

She looked up at him as he watched her conduct her food with his eyebrows raised. "I'm really only good with noodles."

"Just doing cow stuff. How're the colored pencils?"

"Ha, ha, very funny. I get it, there's more than one working part. By the way, when did you get a new truck?" Elijah had escorted Bea to a large, red

Toyota Tundra truck that was very shiny and even more expensive.

"Right after." He didn't say after what. He didn't need to. "Cheaper to buy a new one than fix the old one."

They ate quietly for several minutes, before Bea broke the silence. "I didn't get a chance to thank you for saving my life."

"Glad you were OK," Elijah said somberly, nodding his head.

"Who was that nice man you brought with you? I didn't see anybody's vehicle when I pulled up at the house." Bea slurped another mouthful of noodles.

Elijah stopped eating and looked at her. "I didn't have anyone with me."

"Sure you did. He was older, really nice, kind face. He found me first. I remember he was wearing a light blue shirt and a gray sweater vest thing, like old men wear. I saw him clear as day right before I blacked out. I knew you were there, because he called out to you, and he patted my forehead and said I was going to be all right."

Elijah quit eating and sat there for a few seconds, watching her. "I knew where you were because I heard a man call out. Evelyn and I both did. I thought you'd brought someone."

"Nope." Bea shook her head as Elijah reached for his wallet. He took out an old, tattered picture and unfolded it. There were crease lines down the center, but the faces were plainly visible. In the picture was a much younger Elijah, with an older man. Elijah was wearing a football jersey, and the older man was dressed similar to the man she'd seen.

"Was this him?"

"Yeah, that's him! Who is he?"

"My grandpa. He died in the mine, Bea."

"Oh," Bea said, barely above a whisper. Her memory was fuzzy, and she desperately tried to recall what Elijah had told her. She remembered him saying things to her that night in the hospital room. Mostly, she remembered him saying he didn't want her there. Before her heart broke again, Bea tried to salvage the moment.

"Well, I think he's a guardian angel now. He must've been so proud of you."

"Don't." Elijah shook his head. A one-word sentence. He was starting to shut down again, and Bea knew she couldn't handle it. Instead, she said nothing, and Elijah said nothing, and they ate in silence for the rest of their meal.

When they left the restaurant, Bea suggested they take a walk downtown.

"It's historical. People love it. It's beautiful, too, and it probably won't be crowded since this is a holiday week."

"Sure," was Elijah's only response.

They walked around the grounds of the capitol building, with Elijah barely saying anything.

Her head spun around, trying to figure out the meaning behind his actions. Elijah had driven the three hours from Goodwater Ranch all the way to AU, during one of the most important holidays, yet somehow, she had ended up even more miserable than before.

"How's your portfolio coming along?" Elijah asked randomly, while they walked back to his truck.

"Not good."

"I thought you had everything you needed."

"I scrapped it and started all over." Bea really didn't want to talk about why *Bea in Love* was an epic failure with the man who'd made it that way. "Now it's just a lot of mountain ranges."

"Oh. Why'd you scrap it? What about—" Elijah started.

"I really don't want to talk about it. Can you just take me back, please? I'm getting tired." Bea squeezed her eyes shut, trying to change the last hour into something that would've been memorable for the both of them.

"Sure." He nodded and opened the truck door for her. They drove back to the campus in silence.

Everything was silence. Their whole relationship was silence. All the way back, Bea could only think of all the things Elijah had never told her, and the things that he had told her thinking she hadn't heard. The more she thought, the madder she got. Somehow, this whole epic love story had turned into a tragedy, and she just couldn't handle it anymore.

"I heard you," she finally said out loud, her thoughts bubbling to the surface.

"Didn't say anything."

"No, that night. I heard a lot of what you said in the hospital room. And I just have to say, it doesn't even make sense. You're too kind, and sweet, and gentle. You'd never hurt a soul. I'm sorry that all of that stuff happened to you, but you didn't deserve any of it, and you one-hundred percent didn't cause those events. That much I know for sure. You're not a murderer. You're just a man a lot of crap has piled on top of. I know you think everything is your fault, but it isn't. There may be a lot of bad spirits around Goodwater Ranch, but your grandpa isn't one of them or he wouldn't have helped you find me. That's a fact."

She slapped her knee because she wasn't standing up and therefore couldn't stomp the ground. "Just because you don't want to talk about it doesn't mean I don't have something to say. So there. Now, I've said my piece."

"Your grandma said the same thing."

"Well, she is not wrong," Bea pronounced every word while she smoothed out the invisible wrinkles in her leggings to keep her hands and mind occupied on some medial task.

Evelyn stuck her head between the seats to provide comic relief and to make sure she hadn't been forgotten about.

Chapter Twenty-Two

Bea kissed Evelyn's forehead before she got out of the truck. Elijah stood there, holding the door open for her. In the ten minutes since Bea's outburst until the point Elijah had parked, they hadn't exchanged any words. Yet. Again. For the billionth time in their relationship.

She walked alongside him, her arm linked with his. They'd had to walk slower, because his foot was bothering him. He hadn't said as much, but Bea had seen him wince as he got out of the truck. She felt guilty for making him take the leisurely stroll around the capitol.

When they arrived in front of her dorm room, Bea's heart squeezed tightly in her chest. She wanted him to say what he really meant, what she'd prayed for, which was that he'd come for her because he loved her. He'd driven all this way to tell her that he missed her and that he needed her in his life. Still, he said nothing.

Bea fought hard to contain her emotions. *Why has he come on Thanksgiving week of all weeks, if he isn't going to say all of those things to me?*

Elijah hovered in front of her, close, but not too close. To end the awkward silence, Bea stuck her hand out. Elijah reached out and reciprocated, looking confused, like he wasn't sure what a handshake even was.

"Thank you for coming up, Elijah. It was great to see you and I really appreciate you taking the time out of your schedule."

He nodded slightly, but made no moves otherwise.

A rebel tear raced down her face before she could catch it. "I can't keep going through this, Elijah," Bea stuttered. "Drive safe."

To conceal the rest of her tears that were already beginning to fall, she squeezed his hand slightly before spinning on her heel and running into the building.

~

Something had gone wrong, but for the life of him, Elijah didn't know what. If he'd been a gambling man, he would've lost, because he didn't know *where* he'd gone wrong. He'd showed up unannounced, opened all the doors for her, and paid for her meal. The one time he'd ventured to put his hand on her back, he'd been sure she'd leaned into his touch. Elijah had assumed incorrectly that that was enough, and that she knew how he felt about her.

He wished right then his grandpa was still around, or that if he were a guardian angel, that he would show up and steer Elijah in the right direction again. Old Man Callahan would have known what to do.

Elijah stood there at the base of the stairs, his head reeling with questions, while he watched the door slowly close.

~

Bea ran up to her room, swimming through the blurry mess of vision to search for anything familiar that would lead her to her destination. She found the elevator, a dark, watery mass of a blob against a wall that she knew wound take her up. There was no way she was going to even attempt the stairs in this condition.

The elevator doors closed, and Bea wailed.

Why?

Why did she have to be in love with a Neanderthal? An emotionally crippled, stunted man who had no feelings for her except to just string her along and play with her emotions like that.

Why did she have to feel so deeply and love so bravely as to fall in love with the emotional equivalent of a paperweight?

Bea stumbled to her room, and over to the kitchenette. She searched through her cabinets frantically. She needed something, and there was nothing in her dorm room strong enough to mend a severed heart.

She filled her teapot with water and dropped several chamomile bags in it. It wouldn't do the trick, nowhere close, but at least the smell would make her smile through her tears.

She set the pot on her hot plate, and turned it up to high while she watched and waited for the steam to rise up and consume her grief.

The door slammed behind her. She ignored it, assuming it was just her roommate. A low growl came from behind her and snaked through the steam that was rising into her nostrils.

"Damnit, woman."

Which was the most romantic thing Elijah could think to say. *Isn't that what Rhett had said to Scarlett?* He'd watched *Gone with the Wind* in twenty- to thirty-minute increments, just for her. Just so he could tell her he'd seen it, too.

Her heart squeezed in her chest. "Damnit, man," she said redundantly, not daring to turn her head and break the illusion.

Tears were falling through the top of her teapot, slicing through the smoke that was floating up.

Elijah sighed behind her. "I've done everything I can think of, and I did it all wrong. Do you want me or not?"

Bea looked up at the cabinet, willing her eyes to focus before she dared herself to even look in his direction. She walked over to the sink to grab a towel. She ran cold water over it to blot her eyes quickly, because she was the ugliest of ugly criers.

Elijah watched her silently, patiently, while she took her time to calm down.

Bea turned to him, her face red and splotchy, her eyes bloodshot and shimmery. "Do I want you?" she croaked, her voice raspy with emotion.

He walked over to her, his slight limp making her tears reappear and fall even harder at the guilt that she'd caused him to be in physical pain that day.

Elijah closed the distance between them, caging Bea against the sink with nowhere to escape. Not that she ever would've wanted to.

Through the thin cotton of her T-shirt, the mother of pearl buttons on his plaid shirt pressed against her. The taut muscles contained behind them threatened to undo her very way of life.

Bea's heart had completely fallen into her stomach, and her intestines now looped themselves around it and held on for dear life. Her eyes traveled slowly up, inch by inch, button by button, until they met the hazel fire that threatened to consume her life force.

Elijah's face was inches away from hers, his lips full and pink and eager. Bea hesitated a moment longer, nothing between them but a breath. Her chin trembled as another rogue tear let loose.

Elijah swiped it away with the pad of his thumb, his hand lingering on her cheek. Bea leaned into his warm touch.

"Do you want me?" he repeated, his voice a low growl that uncoiled every nerve in her body.

This. *This* was everything she'd been waiting for.

She nodded at him, not breaking their eye contact. "I want you."

Elijah's hands traveled to her lower back and pulled her closer into him as his lips descended. Bea tilted her head back, and draped her arms around his neck.

Then, for the first official time, Bea St. Claire and Elijah Callahan kissed.

Epilogue

"You've got to quit kissing me," Elijah mumbled into Bea's mouth.

She leaned back slightly, and rubbed her nose against his. "I absolutely will not. You need to just accept it and move on." Then, she leaned down and grabbed the seat reclining handle, and the two of them went flying backwards. Bea burst into a fit of giggles as they resumed their make-out session. Only this time, Evelyn also joined in. Moving in closer, she started licking Bea and Elijah's faces.

"Get off of me, woman," he said, as he tickled Bea into submission and pushed Evelyn away. "We've got a schedule to keep to. Ben only gets an hour for lunch."

They were in front of The Avocado Taco, and it was nearly time for the noon lunch rush. Bea fell backwards into the passenger seat, glancing over her shoulder at Ben's unmarked car that had already been parked beside Elijah's truck for a good while.

"He said he's got big news," Elijah muttered, as he raised the driver's seat back up into the sitting position.

"Maybe I'd rather be kissing you," Bea said, moving towards him again, but Elijah put his hand up.

"Back it up. He only gets an hour as it is. Big news shouldn't be rushed. We'll barely have time to eat with him."

It was spring break, and Bea was staying in Goodwater Ranch for the week, helping Millie out with the abundance of spring orders that were starting to accumulate with the arrival of tourist season. "I've got to get back to the flower shop anyways."

"You do not. We're eating lunch with Ben," Elijah scoffed.

Bea threw her hands up. "OK, fine, Grumpy McGoo. Let's go."

Ben wasn't hard to spot, because he was the only one wearing a suit in the whole place. Bea looked around, admiring Simone's decorating choices. The walls were lime green, with multi-colored crown

219

molding lining the ceiling. The tables were all glass tops, with industrial-style metal chairs for the center ones and black booths for the tables that lined the walls. Scattered throughout the ceiling were Edison bulb chandeliers. It looked like a steampunk pinata had exploded, and Bea loved it.

"We should redo your kitchen to look like this," Bea said, as they walked through the dining room.

"I forbid it," was Elijah's response.

Ben waved as soon as he saw them, and stood up. "I took the liberty of ordering the taco bar when I, ah, saw that you weren't going to make it on time," he said awkwardly. Bea grinned and held her head up proudly.

"Sounds great, man. Thanks," Elijah said, as he waited for Bea to climb into the booth.

Simone approached, carrying a giant tray on her shoulder. She unfolded her tray table, and dished out before them a huge platter of soft and crunchy taco shells, along with large bowls of Pico de Gallo, sour cream, salsa, guacamole, shredded cheese, carnitas, and shredded chicken.

Then, carefully and proudly, she set down a large

bowl of queso. Cilantro leaves were delicately arranged on the top in the shape of a heart. Simone watched for Bea's reaction, but before anyone noticed anything, Ben took a tortilla chip and scooped straight through the middle, ruining her food art. He shoved the chip, dripping with gooey goodness, into his mouth and Simone rolled her eyes.

"OMG, do you have to be such a troll? Scoot over," she said, as she sat down in the booth, bumping Ben's shoulder with her hip and forcing him to move over.

"What?" Ben said, completely oblivious of the cilantro heart he'd just broken.

"Have we started yet?" Simone asked eagerly, grinning as her eyes darted between the three of them.

Bea swirled guacamole and sour cream onto a soft-shell. "Started what?"

Simone looked at Ben, who just shook his head and gestured for her to go ahead. "Ladies first."

Simone squealed and clapped her hands together. Her eyes sparkled with excitement as she talked.

"OK, so, Bea, do you remember that restaurant I told you I was starting up? Well, I got the funding for it. I had to pull a few old strings, but it finally happened."

Ben snorted in disgust, and Simone ignored him and continued talking. "Soooo, about late Fall-ish I'm estimating, I'm going to need that mural we talked about. It's going on a huge wall. Elijah showed me some of your sketches. I know it's not exactly your medium of choice, but the job is yours if you want it."

"Are you serious? I'd love to!" Bea squealed, and then they both squealed together as Elijah and Ben looked at each other, unsure of what was happening in front of them. Bea glanced at Elijah, and he just smiled and nodded his approval.

Simone cleared her throat. "Ahem. I think Ben had something he wanted to say as well." She elbowed him in his ribs to get his attention, because he was focused on alternating layers of carnitas and jalapeños. "Ben?"

"What? Oh, right. *The Goodwater Gazette* was wanting to redesign their logo. I heard they were asking around for some fresh eyes, and I may or may not have given them your name. The editor-in-chief is expecting your call first thing tomorrow morning. I think he'd like to set up an interview. There are no other applicants that I know of, so the job's basically yours." He shoved a taco into his mouth.

"And?" Simone asked impatiently. "Wasn't there something else you were telling me when you got here?"

Ben nodded his head furiously, as jalapeño juice oozed down his chin. He held his index finger up for them to give him a second. Simone rolled her eyes and Elijah snickered. Ben wiped his mouth and took a long drink of water.

"And, the courthouse needs a sketch artist. Full-time. Obviously, I have some pull in that area, and if you want the job, you can start the first week of June."

"Sketch artist? Like the people on Court TV? I'd get to draw serial killers and criminals?"

Ben laughed. "Sure. And you could even go through some training with the police department to do suspect sketches from eyewitness testimony. If you decide you want to go further with it, that is. It's a steady job, and it'll be rewarding knowing that you're helping both the victims get justice, and law enforcement deliver justice." He shrugged his shoulders. "I don't know, it could be interesting for you. It's not really artsy, but there are worse jobs to start with."

Bea shifted excitedly in the booth. "Yes! Tell everybody yes! I'm so excited now! I was terrified, because I didn't have any jobs lined up, and now I have three!" She hopped up and down in the booth, and Elijah placed his hand over his mouth to keep from laughing too loudly.

The doorbell chimed, and in walked Millie and Violet. "Hey, ya'll! If it isn't my favorite granddaughter and her fabulous boyfriend!" said Millie. She squeezed Elijah's shoulder, and patted it several times for good measure. Elijah scanned the floor around their feet, and sighed heavily.

"Hey, Grammy, I could've just brought you back something if you'd wanted me to."

"Nonsense, honey. It's good for us old women to get out and take a stroll to rustle our blood around. Besides, I just started craving Simone's world-famous chorizo queso after you left, and then that was all I could think about. You know how it is."

"Sure. Who's watching the library?" Bea's eyes

shifted to Violet.

"What's with the third degree?" Violet snapped. "I don't have to eat ham sandwiches and canned peaches every day for the rest of my life if I don't want to." Violet was notorious for not veering out of her routine. "I can have a fun lunch every so often. Besides, the weather is … great for walking today." Thunder cracked loudly, as if on cue.

Bea's brows furrowed. "I feel like everybody's acting weird." Elijah didn't look at her, and just shrugged.

The doorbell rang again, and in strolled Rhonda and Jerry, rather loudly. "Ben? Ben! Where is he? Did we miss it?" Her eyes frantically searched the restaurant until they found Ben hiding in the corner with his head down, trying to blend into his surroundings. Bea caught Simone's death look towards Rhonda. Simone felt Bea's eyes on hers and her expression immediately softened as she smiled at her.

Rhonda gulped when she realized she'd nearly let the cat out of the bag.

"You're such an idiot," Violet barked at Rhonda out the corner of her mouth.

"Miss what? What were you missing, Rhonda?" Bea asked. Elijah's nostrils flared while his eyes stayed glued to the plate in front of him.

"Why, Simone's famous guacamole of course. I wouldn't miss it for the world, darlin'!" Rhonda's Southern accent grew syrupy thick, like she'd poured a forty-pound bad of sugar straight into it.

"If you're eating guacamole, who's watching the diner? It's lunch rush." Things weren't adding up, and Bea wasn't playing the game well.

"We were slow today, so me and Jerry decided to close up shop and go on a date day."

"That's not a thing. You wouldn't miss out on your lunch sales, Rhonda. Even I know that."

Elijah let out a huge sigh and groaned. "We should go. Looks like everybody just wants to eat appetizers with Simone."

Curious about everyone's behavior, but more eager to make out with Elijah again, Bea nodded and shoved down the last bite of her taco.

"I'm sorry," Rhonda mouthed to Elijah after Bea had passed by her.

As soon as Bea hopped up into the truck, she heard a jingle. Evelyn stuck her head between the seats to see if Bea had bothered to bring her a snack. Elijah climbed into the driver's side seat, and another jingle sounded.

"What's that sound?" Bea asked, looking around the outside of the truck. "I don't see anything."

"Must be her collar." Elijah shifted in the seat to where his body was halfway facing towards Bea.

Bea flipped the visor down and put her sunglasses on, even though it was gloomy outside. "The sun will pop out any minute. I can feel it in my skin cells," she explained to Elijah, even though he hadn't asked. "Evelyn doesn't wear a collar. Never has, as long as I've known her."

"Looks like she went shopping while we were inside."

Bea set her glasses on the top of her head and glanced at him. He just raised his eyebrows and nodded towards Evelyn. Bea turned her body fully around to the side, and looked at the bell and the black velvet box that was hanging from Evelyn's neck.

Bea's initially shocked expression turned to a megawatt smile in a matter of seconds. "What's that?"

Elijah reached towards the dog and unfastened her collar. "Thought you'd like it if I did it in front of everyone. Didn't go as planned."

Bea looked at The Avocado Taco, where everyone she knew in town was plastered against the window in the corner, watching them and eagerly awaiting a sign.

"You did all this? This whole plan?"

"Had some help," he said with a shrug.

"This is adorable, Elijah. This is the cutest thing ever. I'm overwhelmed with the cuteness!" Bea's smile hadn't faltered even a millimeter since seeing the ring box.

"Wasn't going for cute, so much as a representation of my undying devotion."

"I love it. I love it all. It's adorable!" Bea squealed.

"Can I ask, or are you gonna keep talking about how adorable everything is? You're ruining the moment." He was rubbing his forehead and trying not to get too tickled at her enthusiasm.

"Nope. I'm mean, yep, go ahead. I'm ready." Bea straightened up in her seat, and held her head high. She waved her palms out in front of her. "You may proceed."

"Albuquerque St. Claire, will you marry me?"

Bea looked at him, puzzled. She tilted her head to the side. "Wait, that's it? Where's your speech? I have to say no to this." She shook her head, her ponytail swishing back and forth in rhythm.

"No? You have to say no? That's the gold standard question."

"Yes. No."

"You can't say no. I just got you three jobs. That you accepted, by the way."

Bea shook her head. "No. You need to say something else first. This is unacceptable." She crossed her arms.

Elijah started laughing, a deep, hearty laugh at her. "All right. What would be acceptable?"

She shrugged and puffed out her bottom lip. Elijah

tapped his chin while he thought. "Got it."

"Go on. Everyone's waiting." Bea side-glanced at the group in the window. "Can't let the audience down, Callahan."

"You're a pain in the ass."

Bea huffed. "Um, try harder to win me over?"

"You're a pain in the ass," he repeated, raising his finger as Bea opened her mouth to protest. "But, don't even for a minute think I haven't been madly in love with you since you broke into my house and went all TLC on it."

"You seriously just used the term 'all TLC'? I'm rubbing off on you. Go on, you're getting better."

"You get me when nobody else in this town does. You're the sunlight in all of my storms." He rolled his eyes at the fact that he had just used such a cheesy line.

"Why?"

"Why what?"

"Why? Simple question."

Elijah rolled his eyes. "Because, woman. Because

I'm yours, and you're mine, and that's just how it is. There's not an alternative option here."

"Yes." A solitary tear rolled down Bea's cheek, and her megawatt smile returned.

"Yes? 'Yes' yes, or you accept my speech 'yes'? You didn't even see the ring yet." Elijah opened the box, which held a cushion diamond solitaire on a rose gold filigree band.

Bea wiped the tears from her eyes. "I don't need to. I just got everything I prayed for. 'Yes' yes."

Elijah slipped the ring onto her finger, and Bea threw her arms around his neck. As their lips met, a muffled roar of excitement erupted from the other side of the restaurant's window.

Elijah and Bea's wedding

will conclude in a later book…

Christmas at Goodwater Ranch

I used to have recurring dreams of the same town, where I would explore different parts and meet different citizens of the town. So, I'm going to attempt to recreate that in the *Goodwater Ranch* series.

I love the ideas of small-town series, where you can get to know each character and their individual backstory. So far, I have about twelve books planned out. Most will be in the series itself, a few will be stand-alone novels.

And Ben will get his own spin-off series, that will be more like romantic suspense.

Plus, the last Levander book, and two more in the History of Vampires series. There's a lot happening in my head!

Thank you for taking the time to read The Cowboy! I hope that you fell in love with Elijah and Evelyn as much as I did.

And Rhonda, mercy me. Don't we all know a Rhonda or two? ;)

Also by Amanda Lewis

The Levander Brothers Series

The Weight of Birds (2020 Silver Medal Winner, Contemporary Christian Romance, Reader's Favorite Awards)

Still Waters: Peter's Story

A History of Vampires Series

A History of Vampires – A New Queen

A History of Vampires – Legends & Lore (Pre-order now!)

Goodwater Ranch Series

The Cowboy – A Goodwater Ranch Romance

The Movie Star - A Goodwater Ranch Romance (Pre-order now!)

If you'd like to receive updates, information, character inspirations, exclusive content and short stories, please consider subscribing to my ***The Story Behind the Story*** newsletter!

https://www.patreon.com/theamandalewis

If you'd like to receive FREE e-mail updates when new releases come out, please subscribe at:

https://www.bookbub.com/profile/amanda-lewis

Acknowledgements

I want to thank God first and foremost for this gift and the inspiration for these characters.

Thank you to my husband, my family, and my friends for always being supportive.

Thank you to my unicorn team for being my faithful cheerleaders.

Thank you to Mark, who's worked with me on every book except the first now. Thank you for being consistently awesome.

Thank you to Elizabeth, my new pro teammate for this gorgeous cover and future covers to come!

And last but certainly not least, thank you to all of my readers! I hope you enjoy reading my stories as much as I enjoy writing them! :)